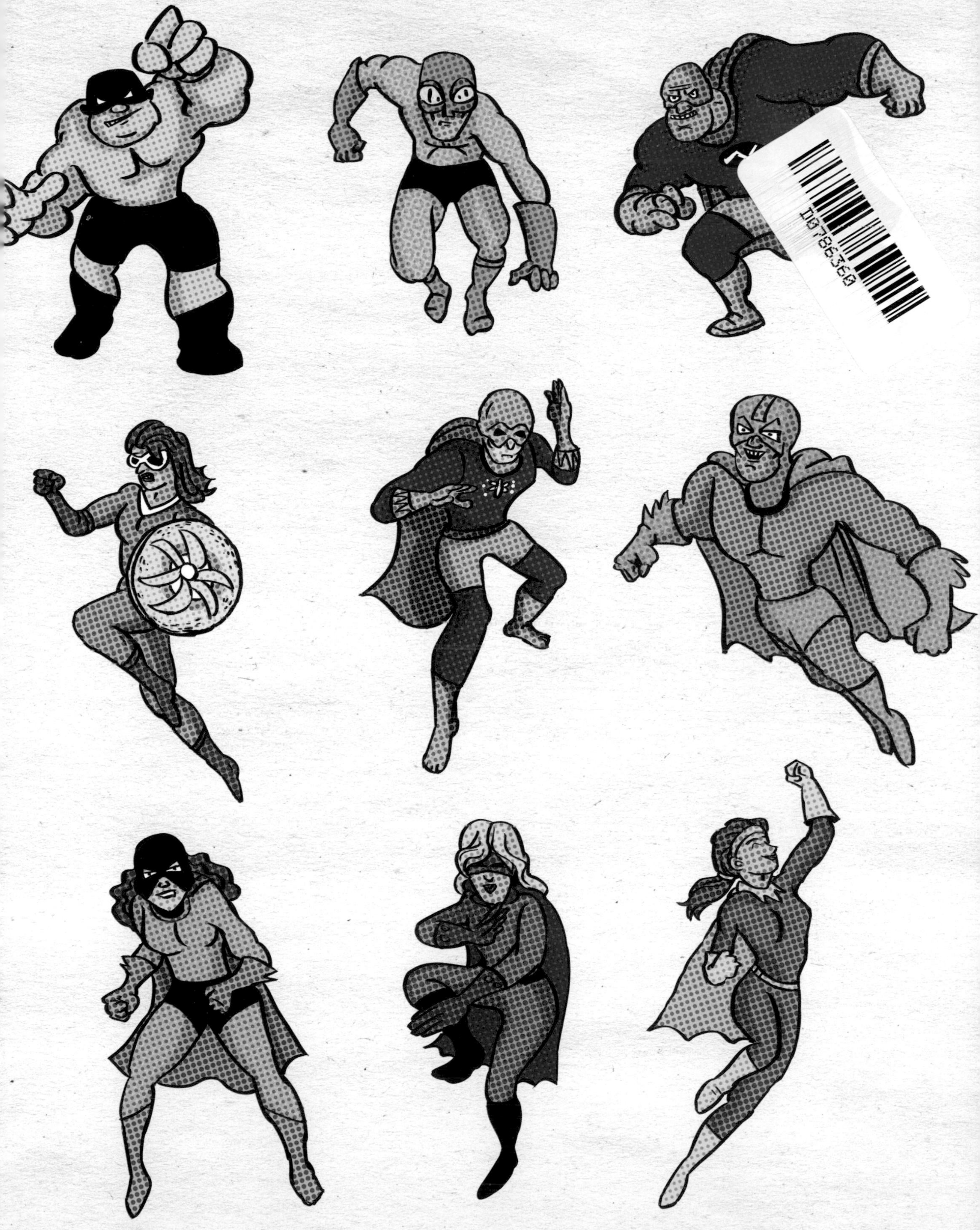

THIS IS A BORZOI BOOK PUBLISHED BY ALFRED A. KNOPF

Text copyright © 2016 by Kristy Dempsey. Jacket art and interior illustrations copyright © 2016 by Mark Fearing.
All rights reserved. Published in the United States by Alfred A. Knopf,
an imprint of Random House Children's Books,
a division of Penguin Random House LLC, New York.
Knopf, Borzoi Books, and the colophon are registered trademarks of Penguin Random House LLC.

Visit us on the Web! randomhousekids.com
Educators and librarians, for a variety of teaching tools, visit us at RHTeachersLibrarians.com

Library of Congress Cataloging-in-Publication Data is available.
ISBN 978-0-385-75534-4 (trade) — ISBN 978-0-385-75535-1 (lib. bdg.) — ISBN 978-0-385-75536-8 (ebook)

The illustrations in this book were created using pencil and digital color.
MANUFACTURED IN MALAYSIA
May 2016   10 9 8 7 6 5 4 3 2 1   First Edition
Random House Children's Books supports the First Amendment and celebrates the right to read.

For my nephews:
Drew, Mac, Mills, and Zae,
who are super
without even trying.
—K.D.

For Jace and Lena,
two super kids!
—M.F.

SUPERHERO
INSTRUCTION MANUAL

by **Kristy Dempsey**

illustrated by **Mark Fearing**

ALFRED A. KNOPF
New York

Do you have what it takes to be a hero and **save the world**?

Are your muscles made of **elastic**?

Are your bones made of **steel**?

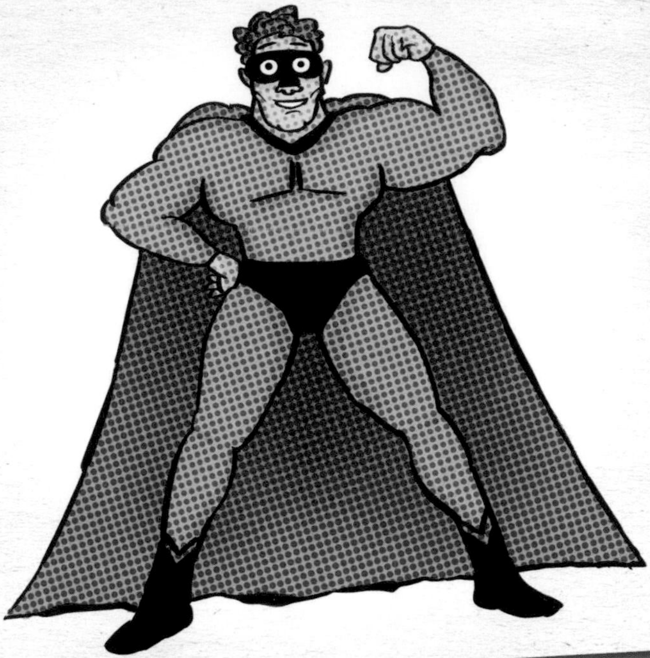

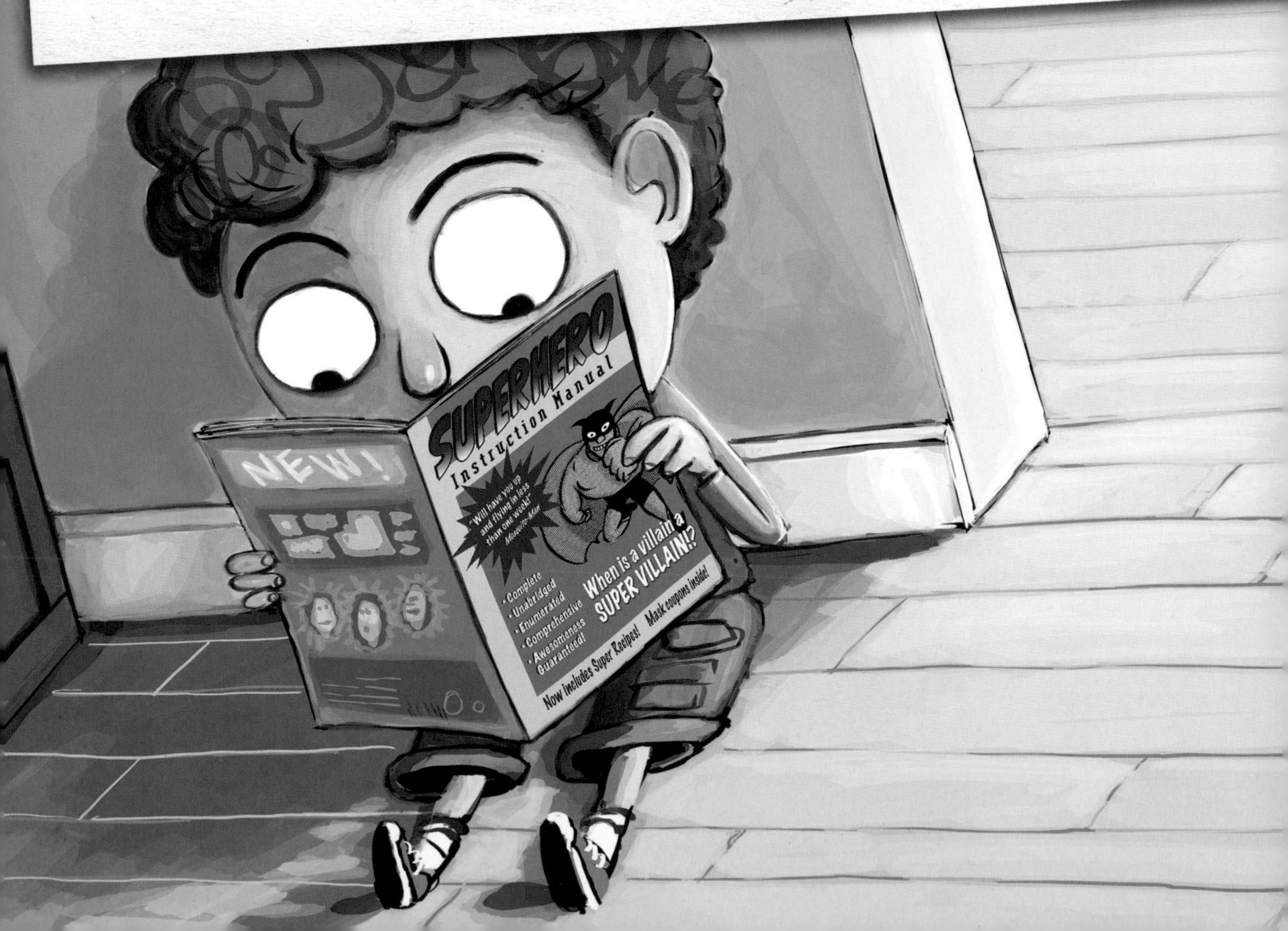
NEW!
SUPERHERO
Instruction Manual
"Will have you up and flying in less than one week!" Mosquito-Man
• Complete
• Unabridged
• Enumerated
• Comprehensive
• Awesomeness Guaranteed!
When is a villain a SUPER VILLAIN!?
Now includes Super Recipes!
Mask coupons inside!

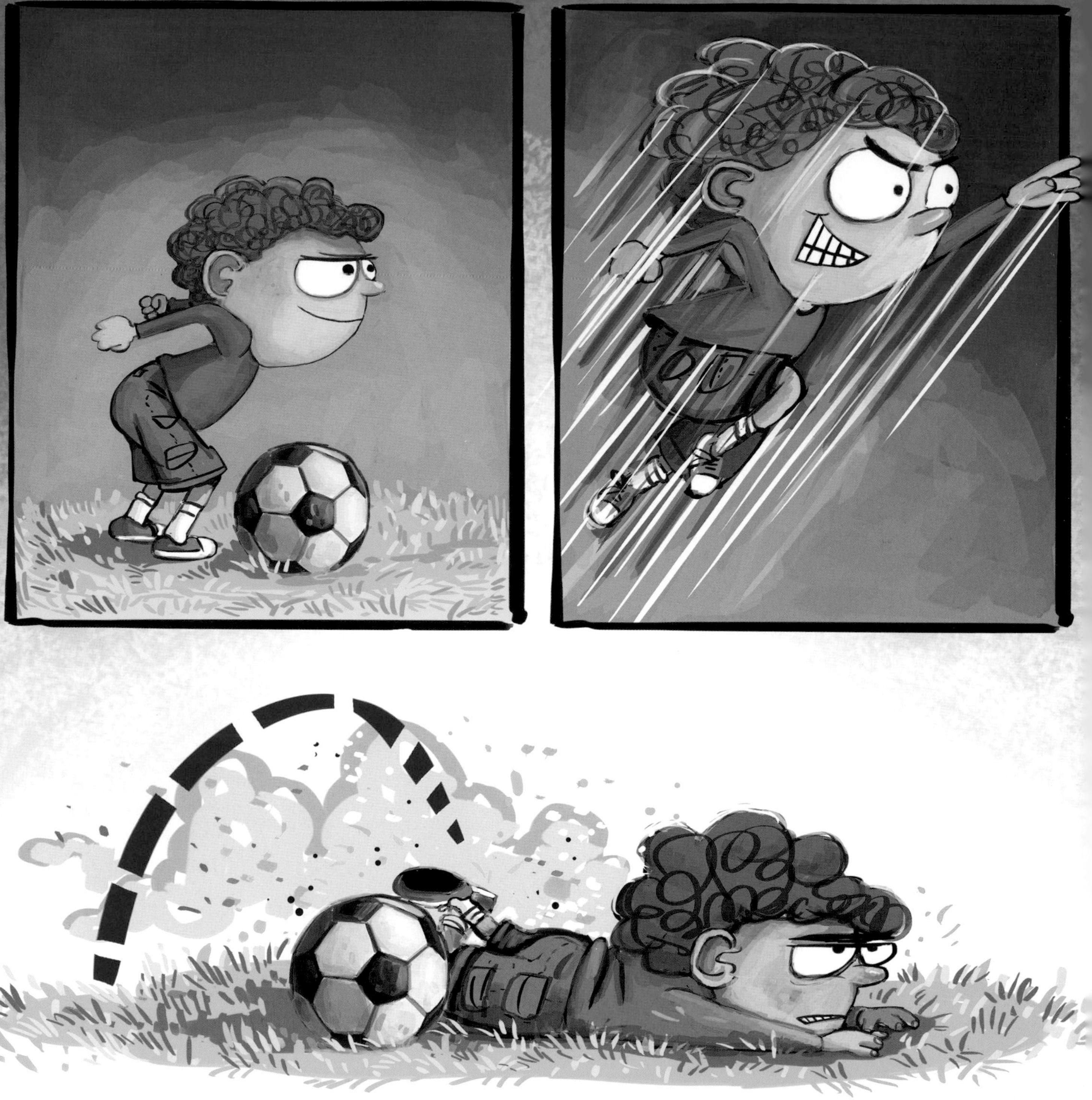

Can you **soar through the air**
with a single leap?

Never fear. Our one-of-a-kind

SUPERHERO Instruction Manual

will turn you super in

seven easy steps.

STEP 1: CHOOSE A SUPER NAME

Need help? Combine your favorite color with your favorite animal. Be the Green Tiger. Or the Pink Python. With two little words, you even *sound* super!

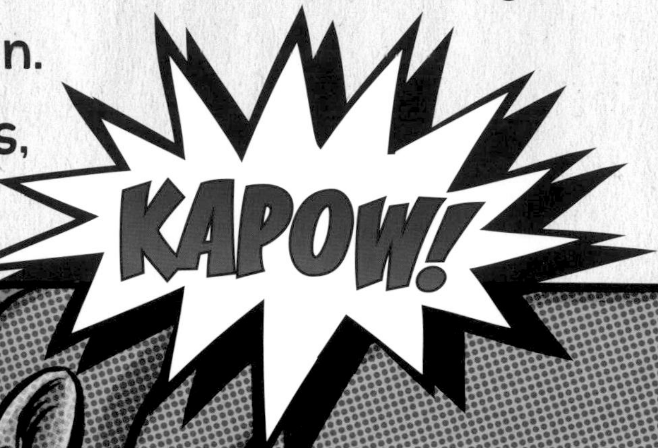
KAPOW!

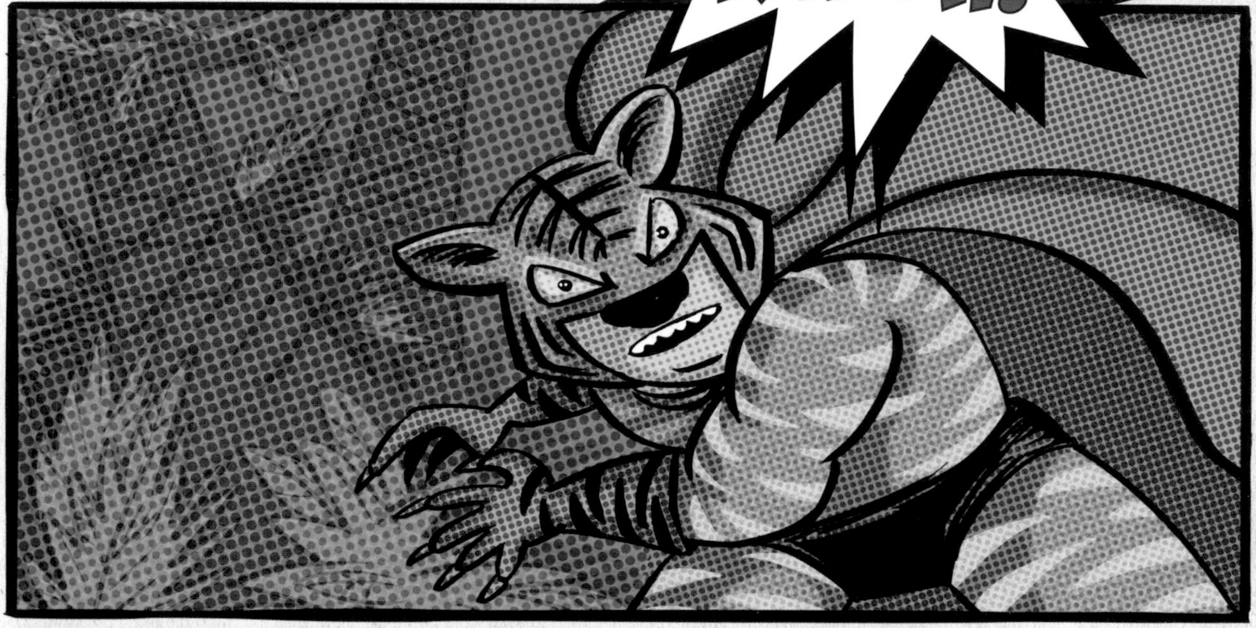

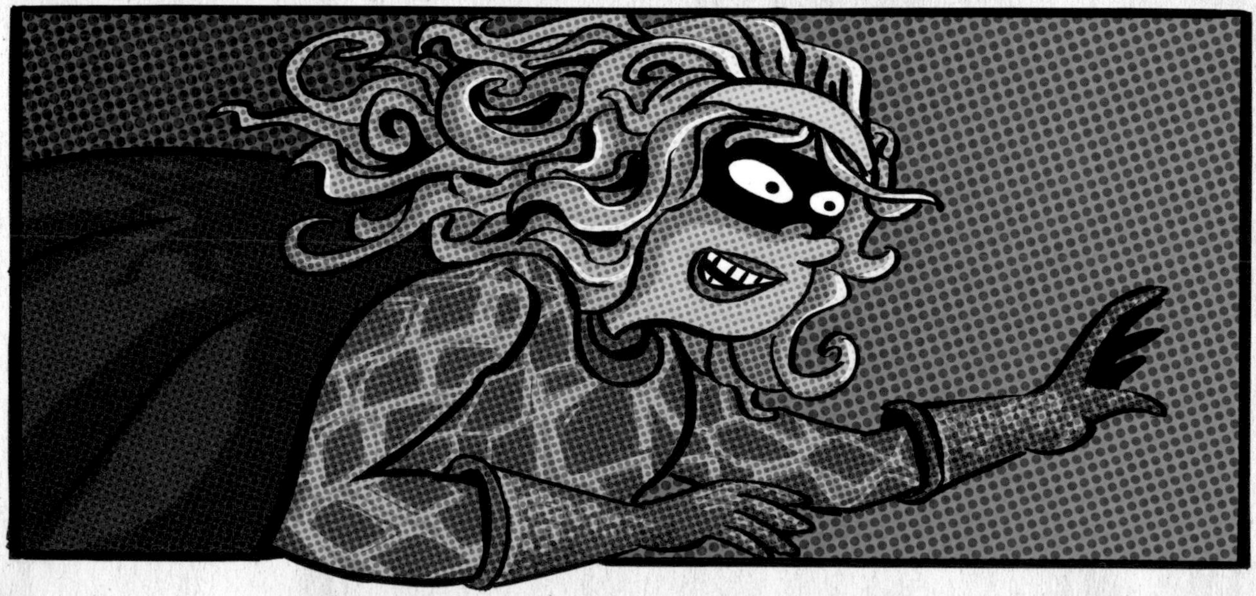

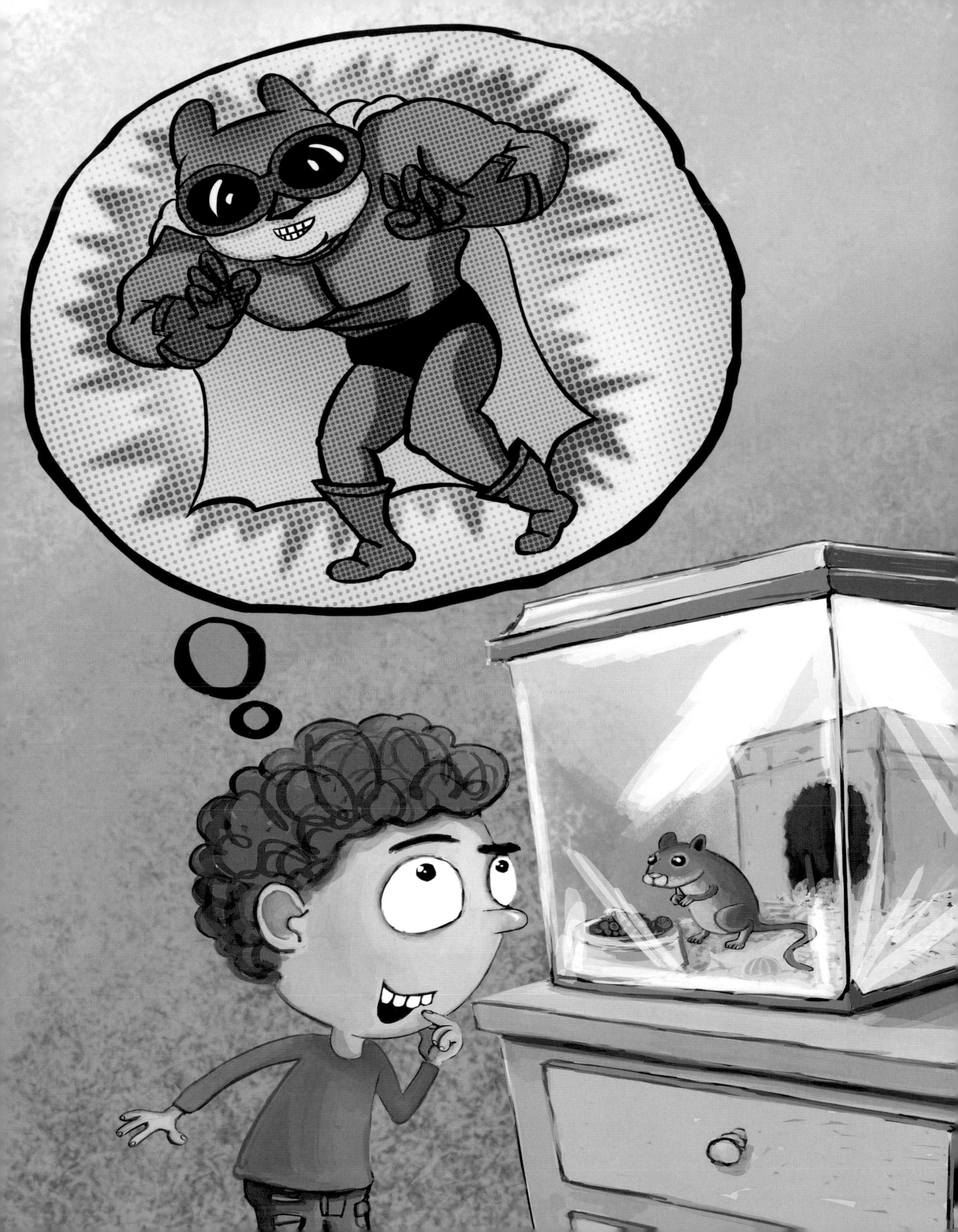

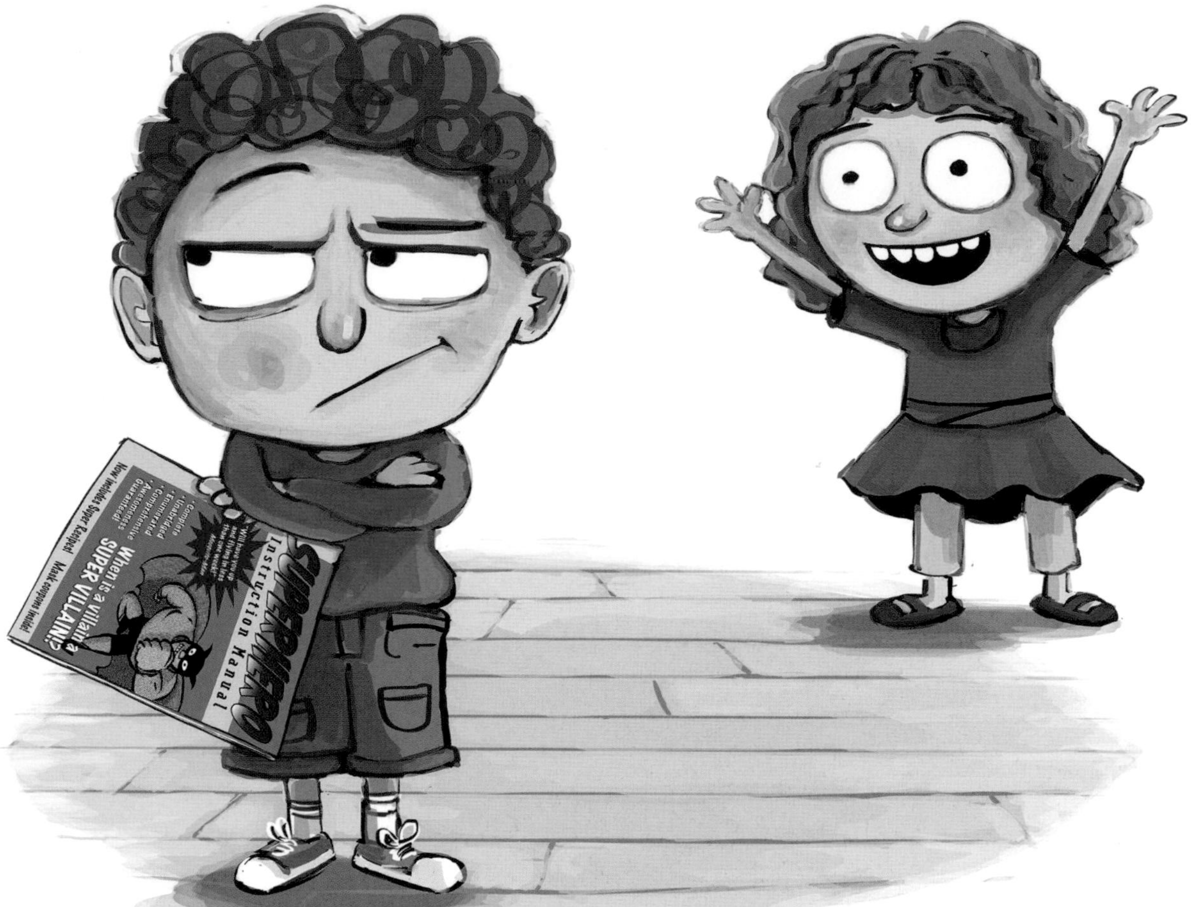
SUPERHERO
Instruction Manual
• Complete
• Unabridged
• Enumerated
• Comprehensive
• Awesomeness Guaranteed!
When is a villain a SUPER VILLAIN!?
Now includes Super Recipes!
Mask coupons inside!

STEP 2: PICK A PARTNER

Holy donut, hero! You need a sidekick! Choose wisely. Remember, your sidekick will look up to you and hope to become a hero, too.

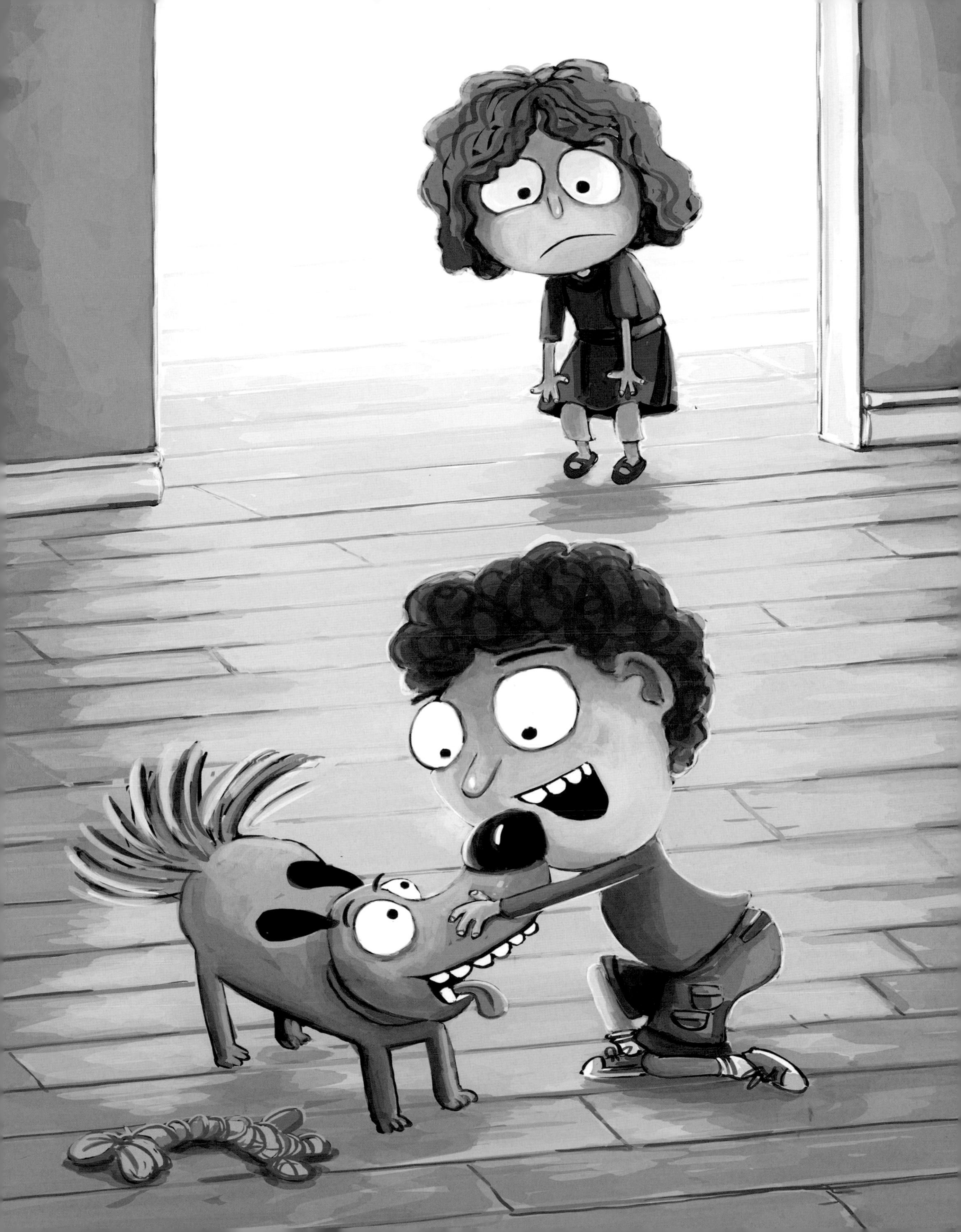

STEP 3: CRAFT A SUPER DISGUISE

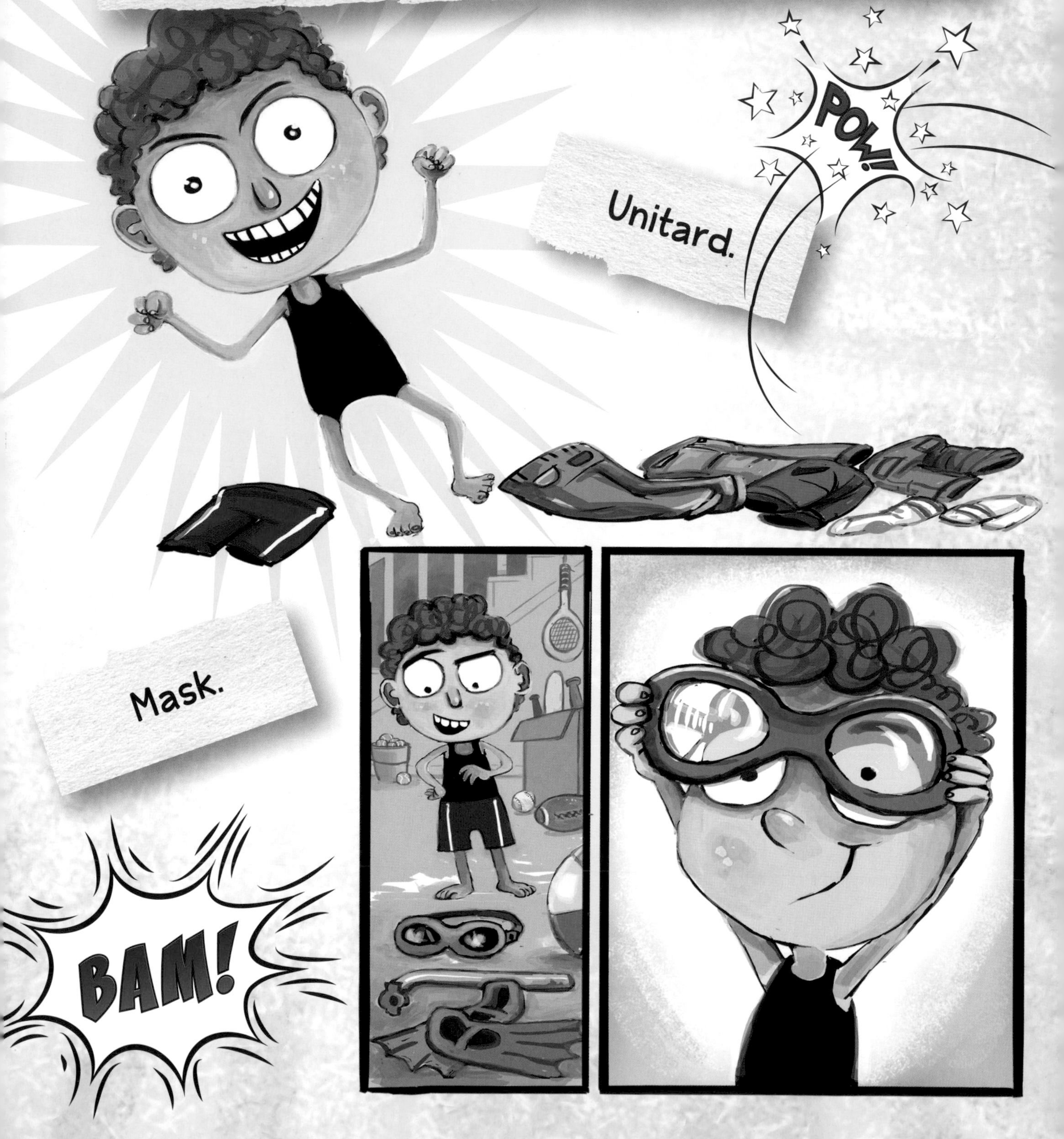
Unitard.
POW!
Mask.
BAM!

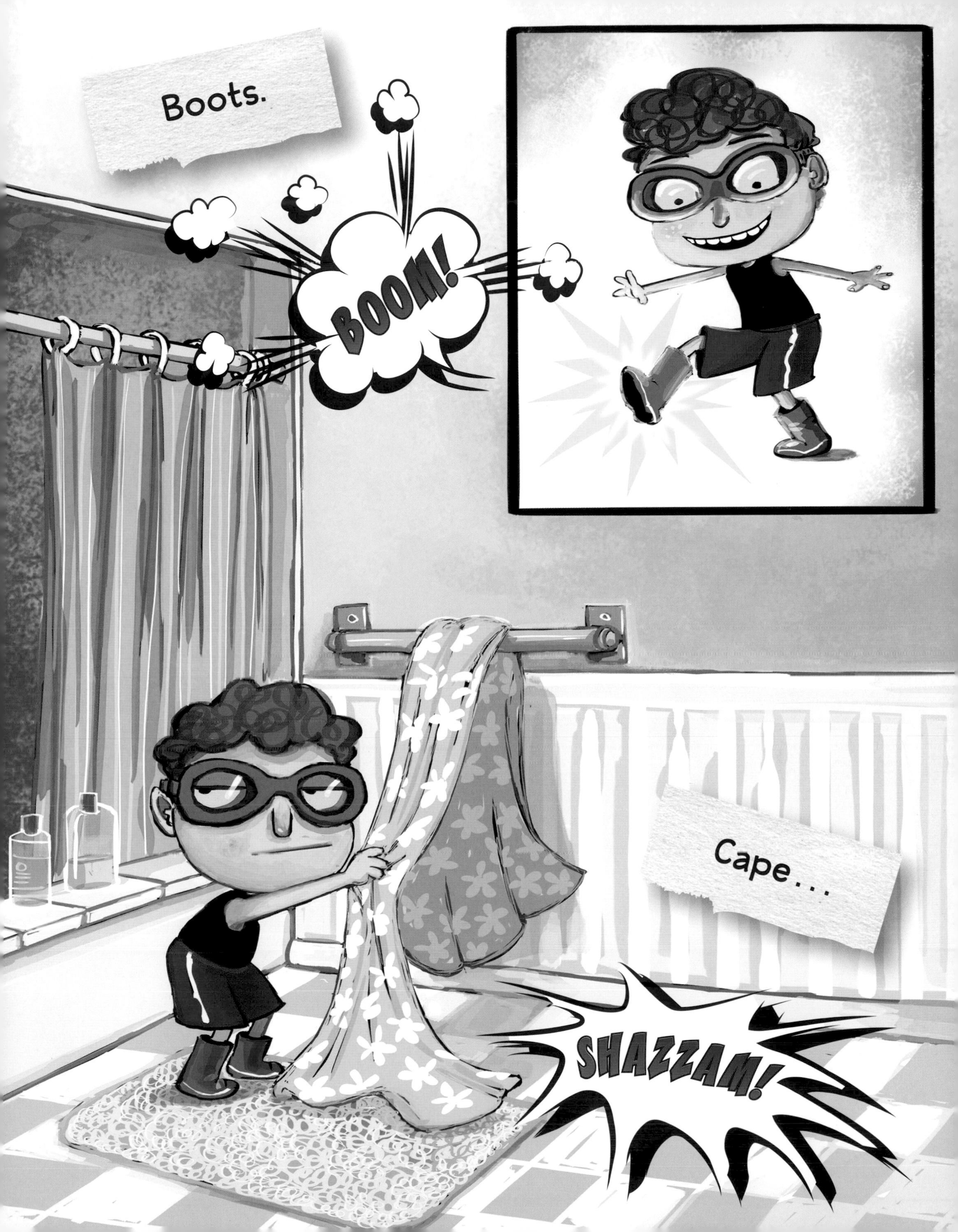
Boots.
BOOM!
Cape . . .
SHAZZAM!

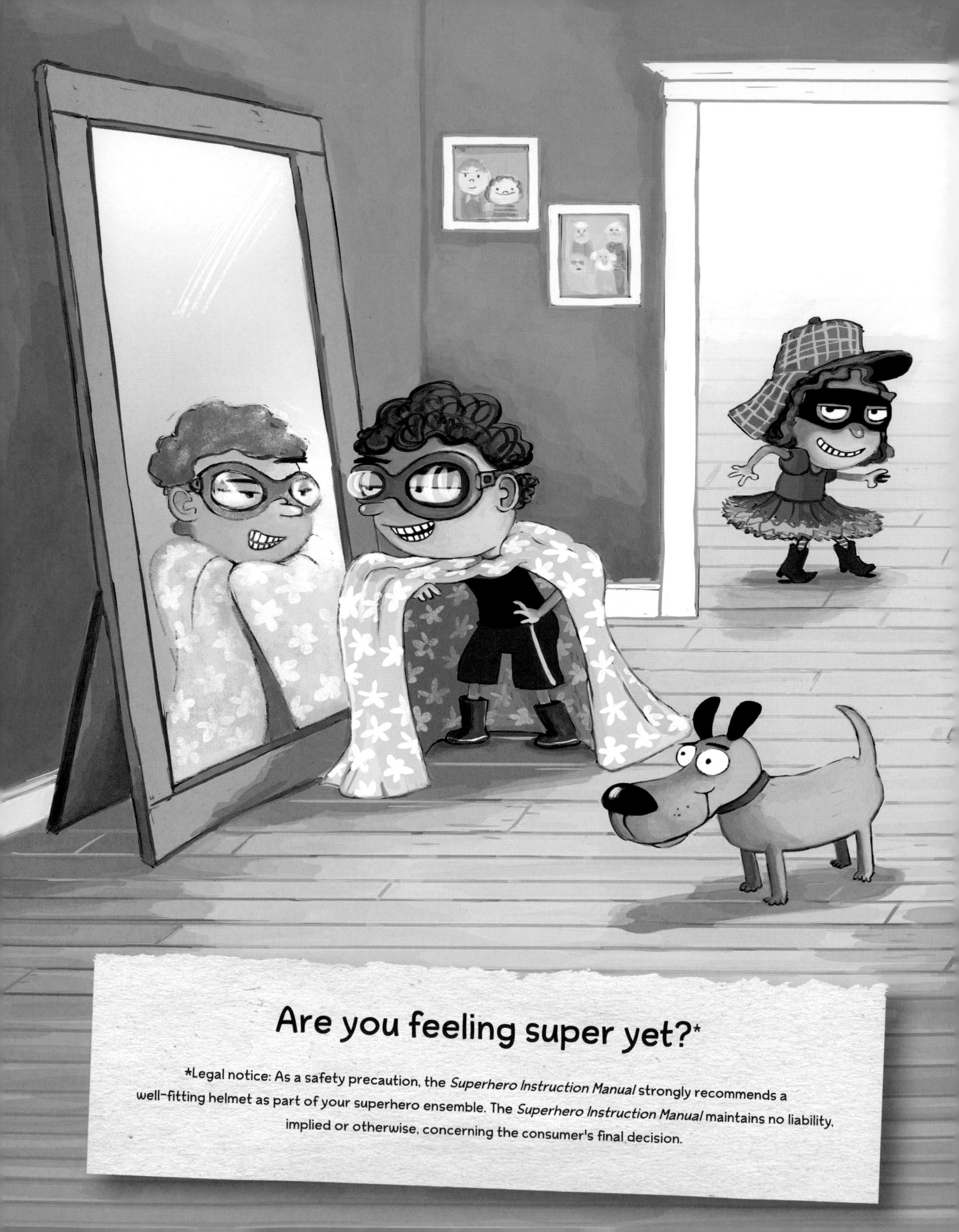

Are you feeling super yet?*

*Legal notice: As a safety precaution, the *Superhero Instruction Manual* strongly recommends a well-fitting helmet as part of your superhero ensemble. The *Superhero Instruction Manual* maintains no liability, implied or otherwise, concerning the consumer's final decision.

STEP 4: SECURE A SUPER HIDEOUT

Every superhero needs a secret lair to plan strategy and prepare to save the world.

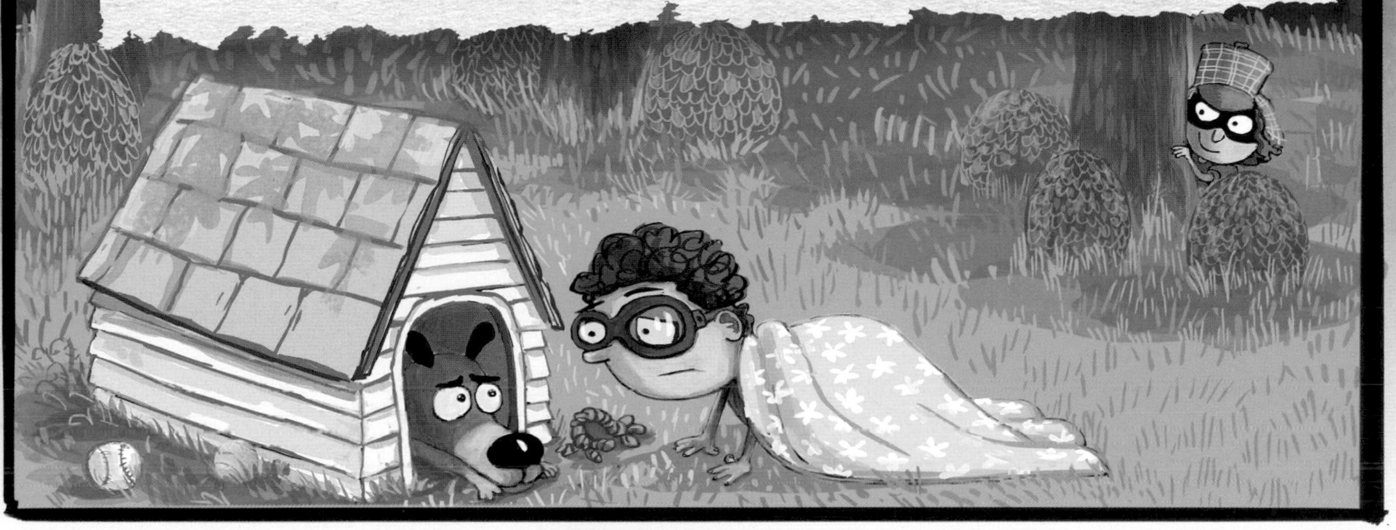

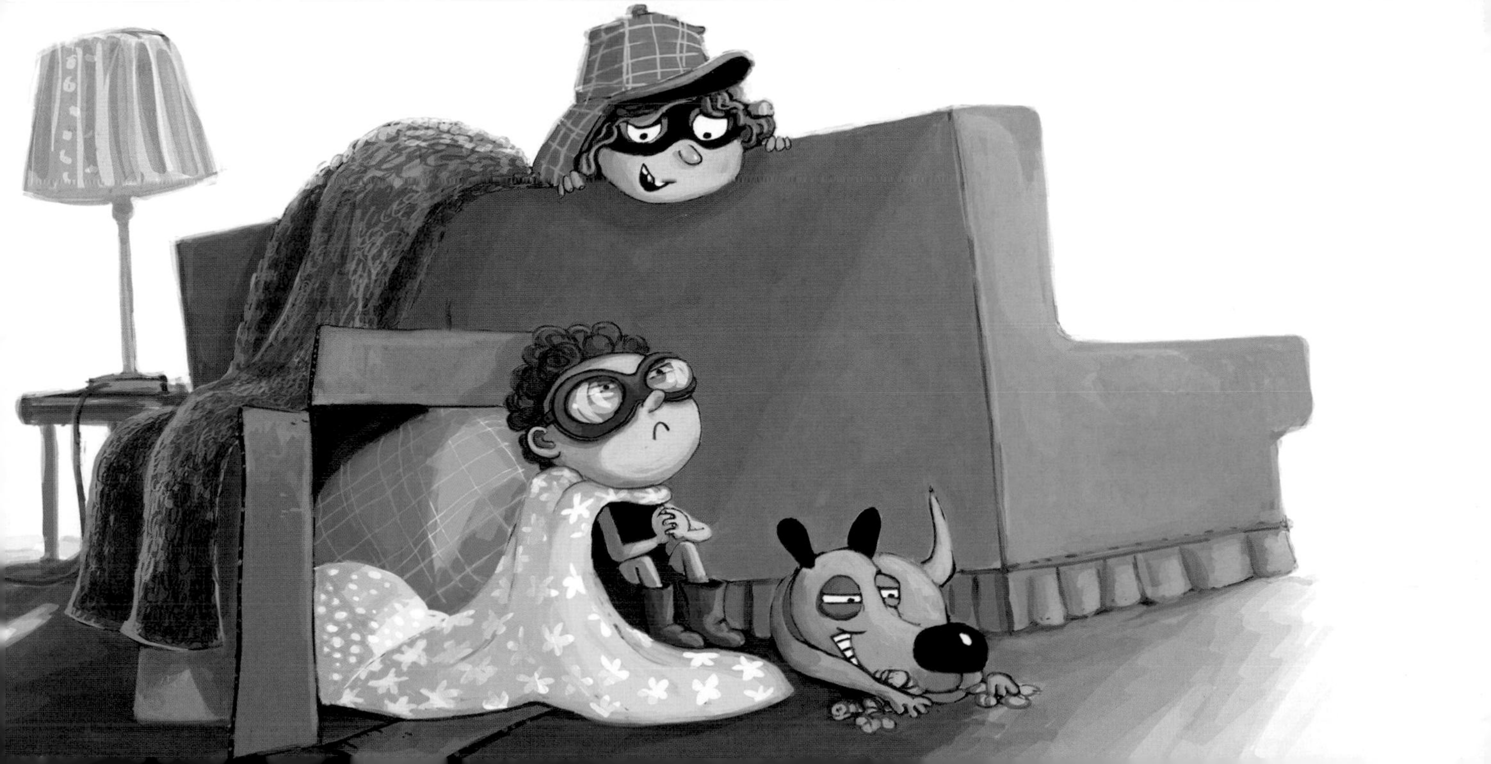

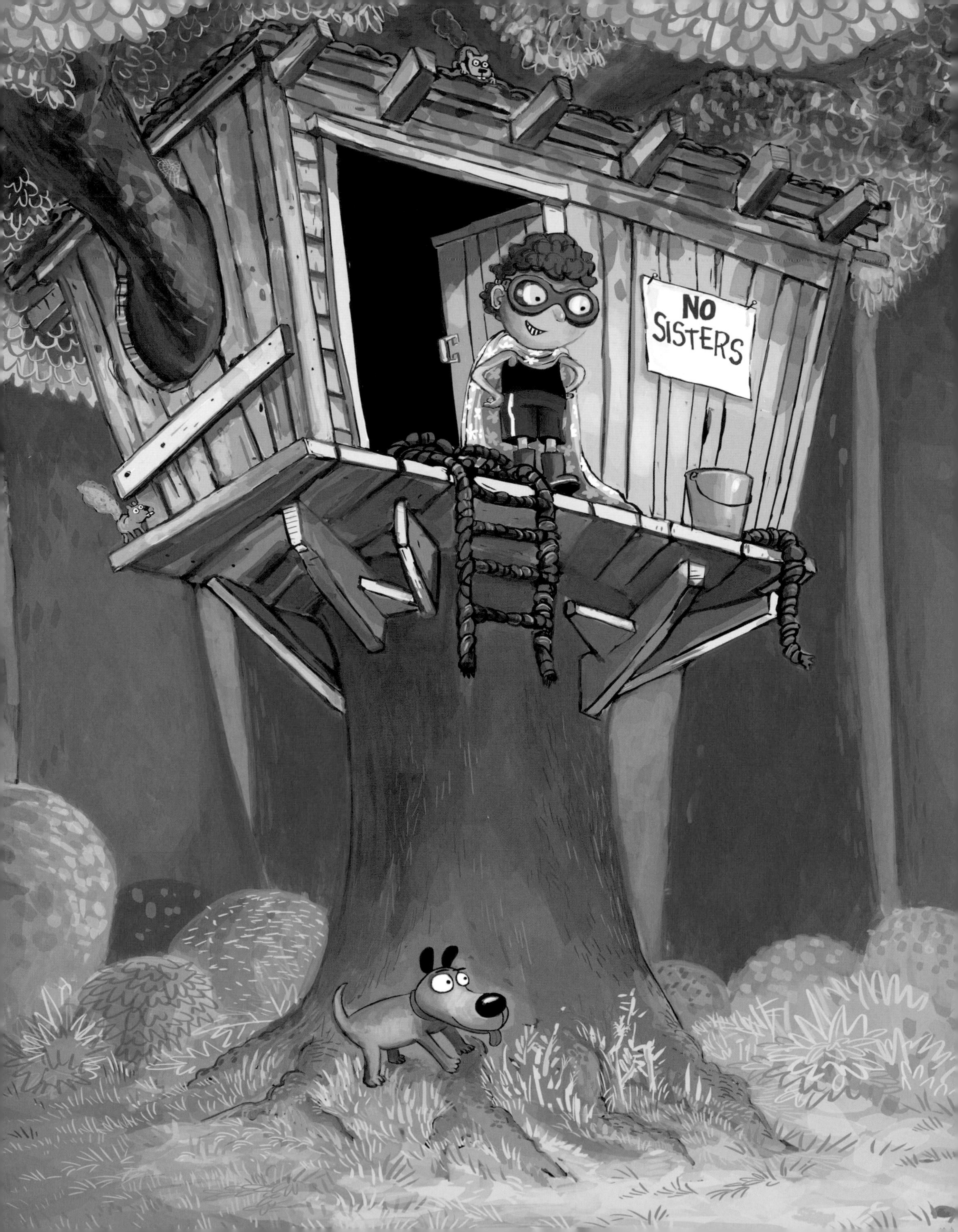
NO
SISTERS

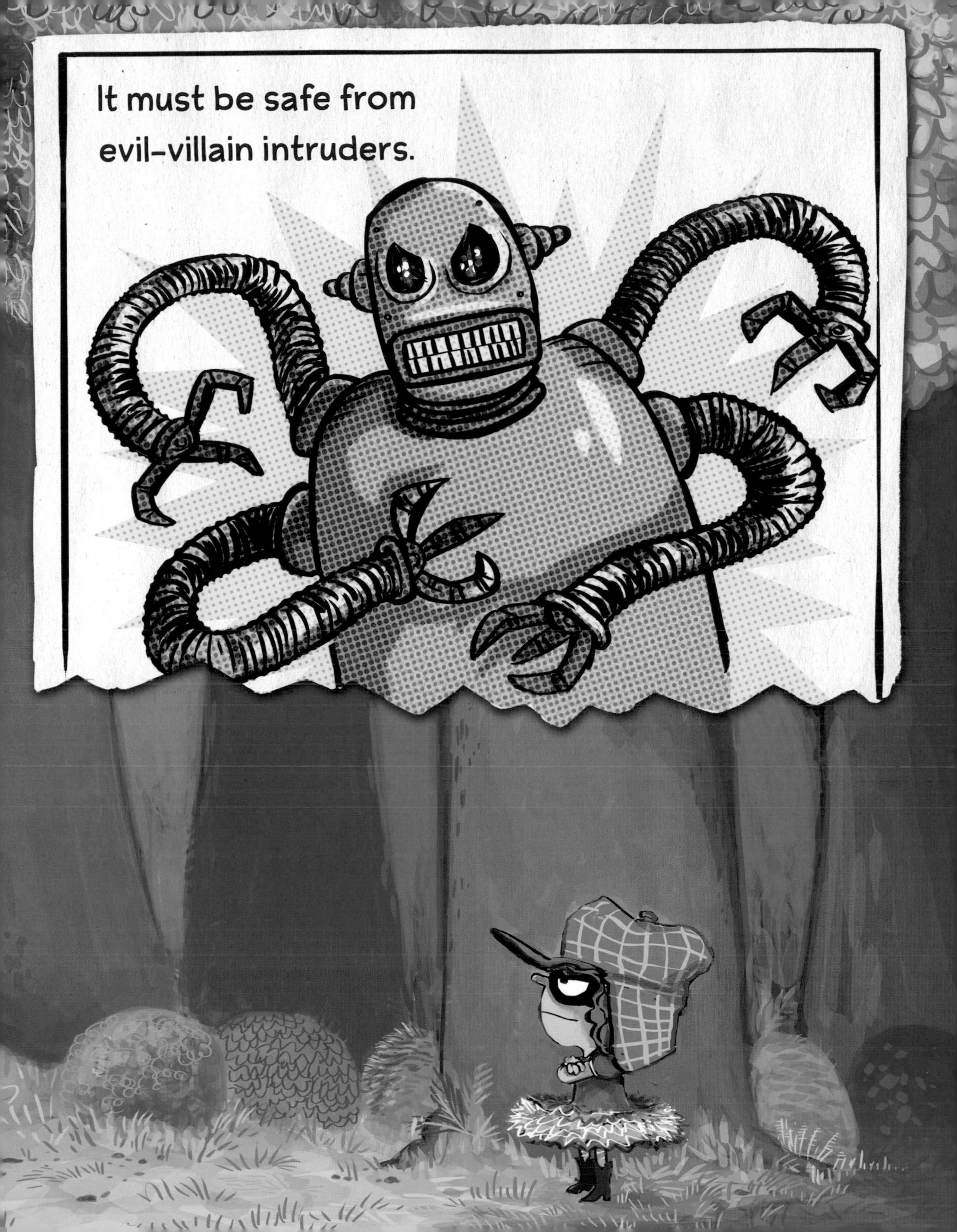
It must be safe from
evil-villain intruders.

STEP 5: CHOOSE YOUR SUPERPOWER

Superheroes don't just wake up one day with amazing powers.**

**Okay, okay. Sometimes a normal human gets a radioactive-spider bite and wakes up with super skills. But that's rare.

You must work hard to discover your inner ***BAM-BOOM-POW!***

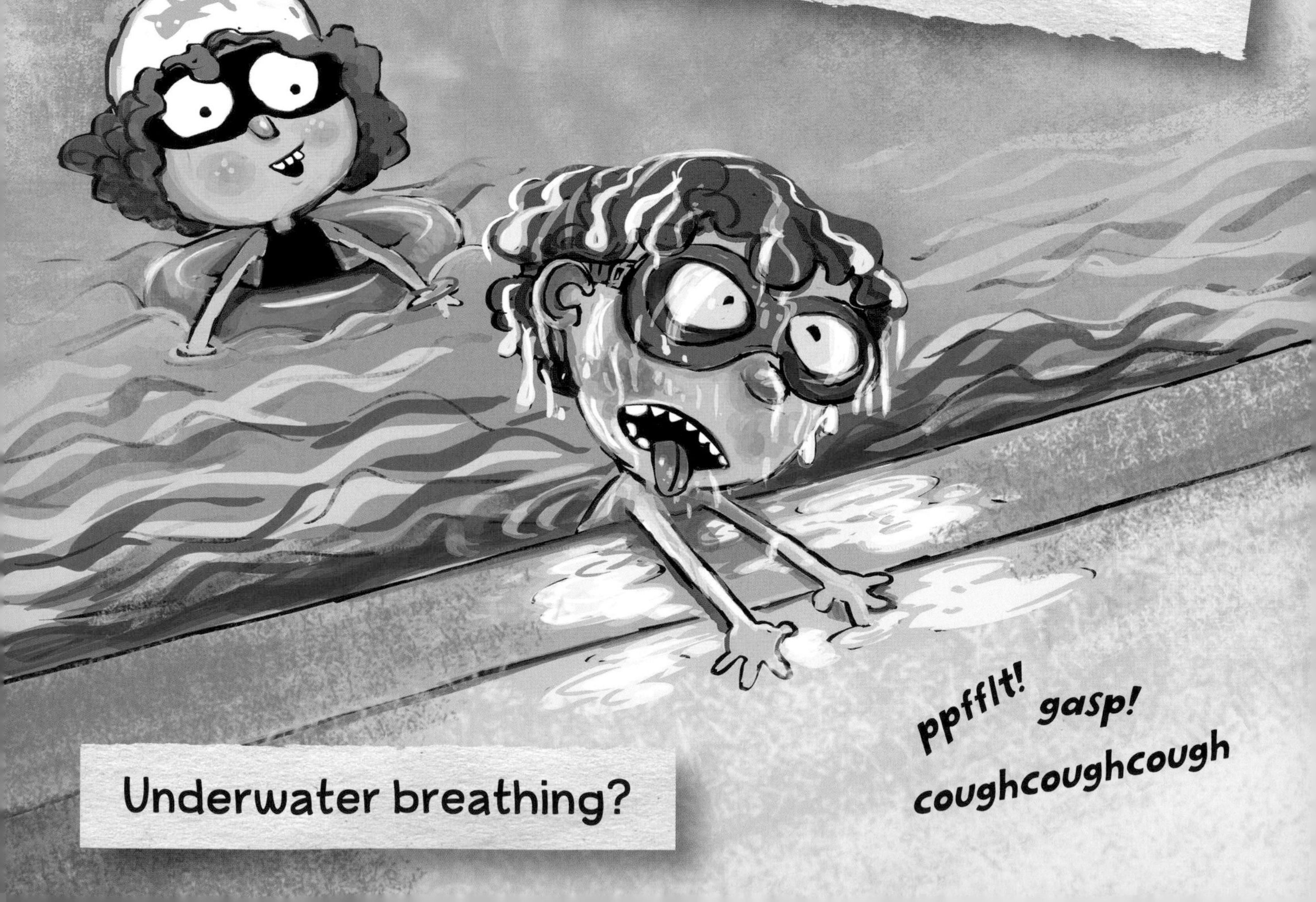
ppfflt!
gasp!
coughcoughcough

Underwater breathing?

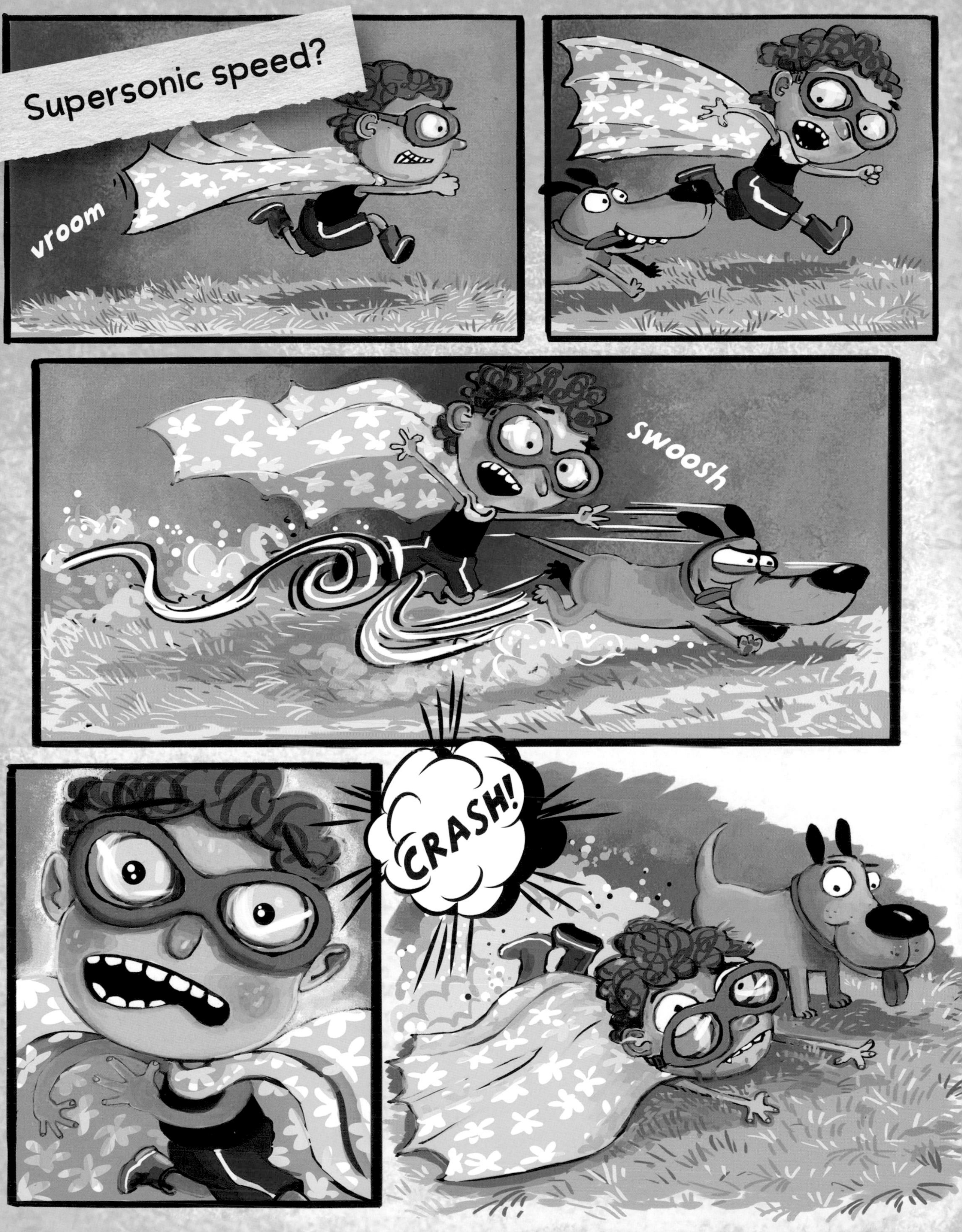
Supersonic speed?
vroom
swoosh
CRASH!

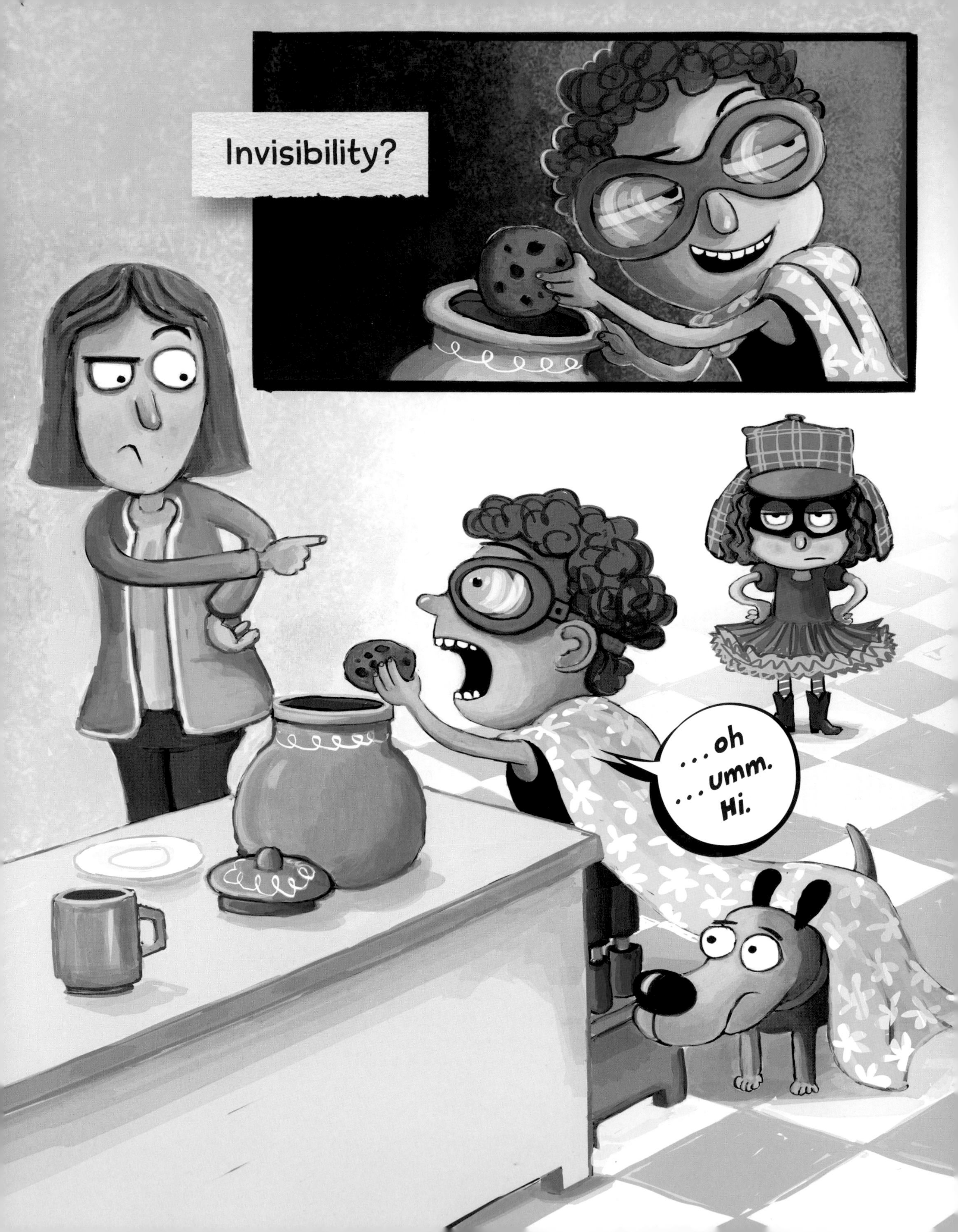
Invisibility?
...oh
...umm.
Hi.

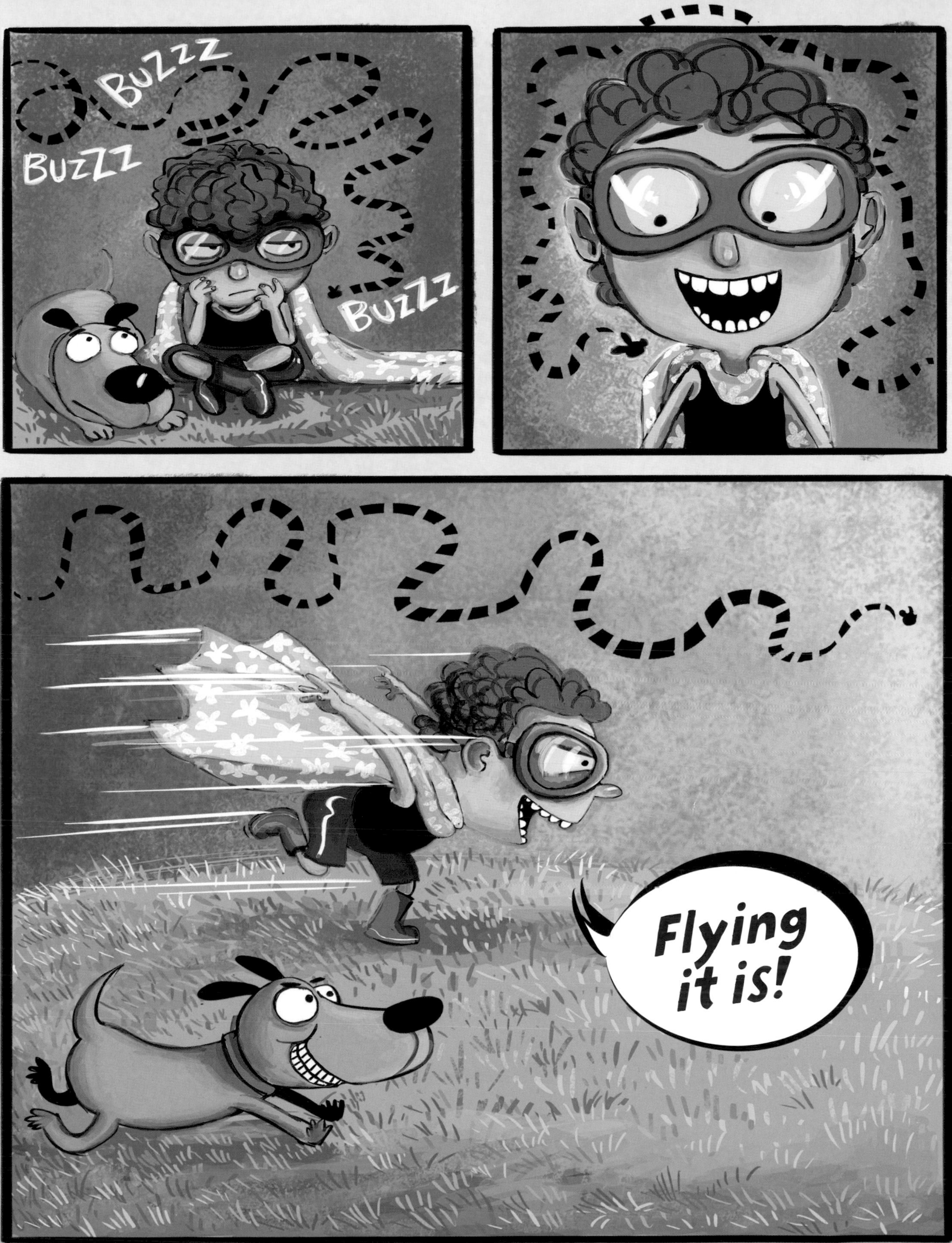
BUZZZ
BUZZZ
BUZZZ
Flying it is!

STEP 6: STORE UP SUPER ENERGY

Being super requires a LOT of power.
Be sure to mega-size breakfast . . .

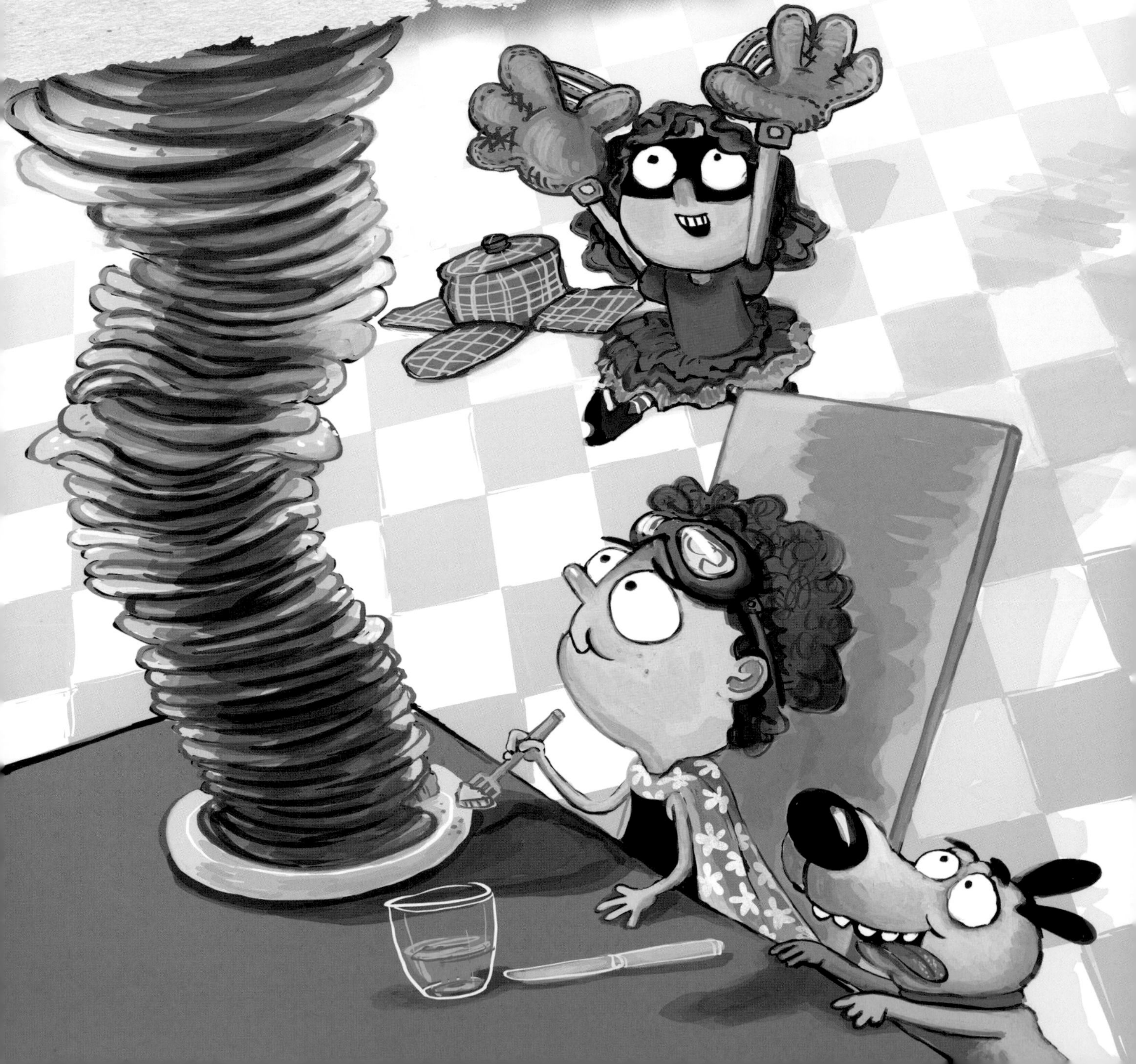

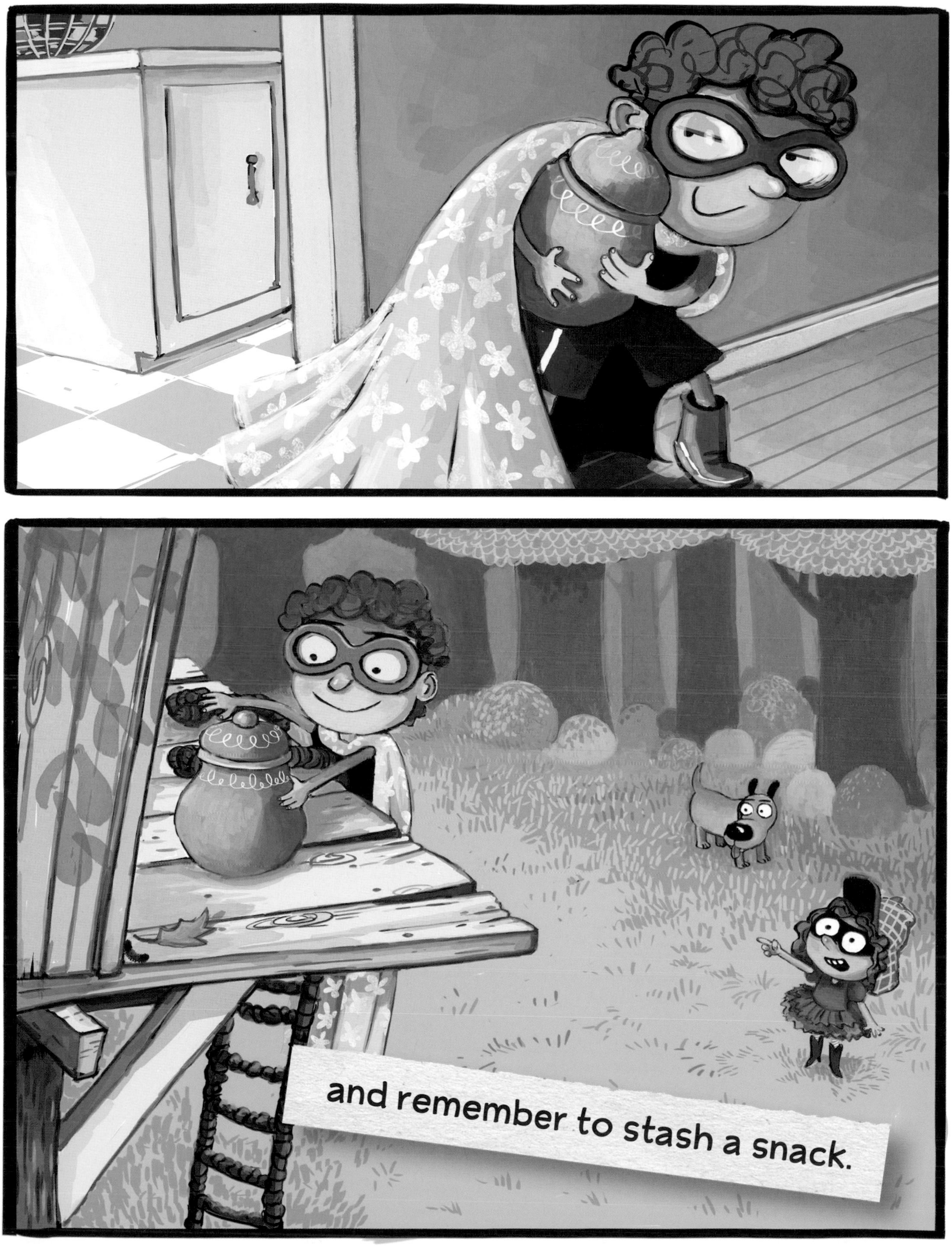
and remember to stash a snack.

STEP 7: SAVE THE WORLD!

It's time to take action, hero!
Show the world what you're made of.

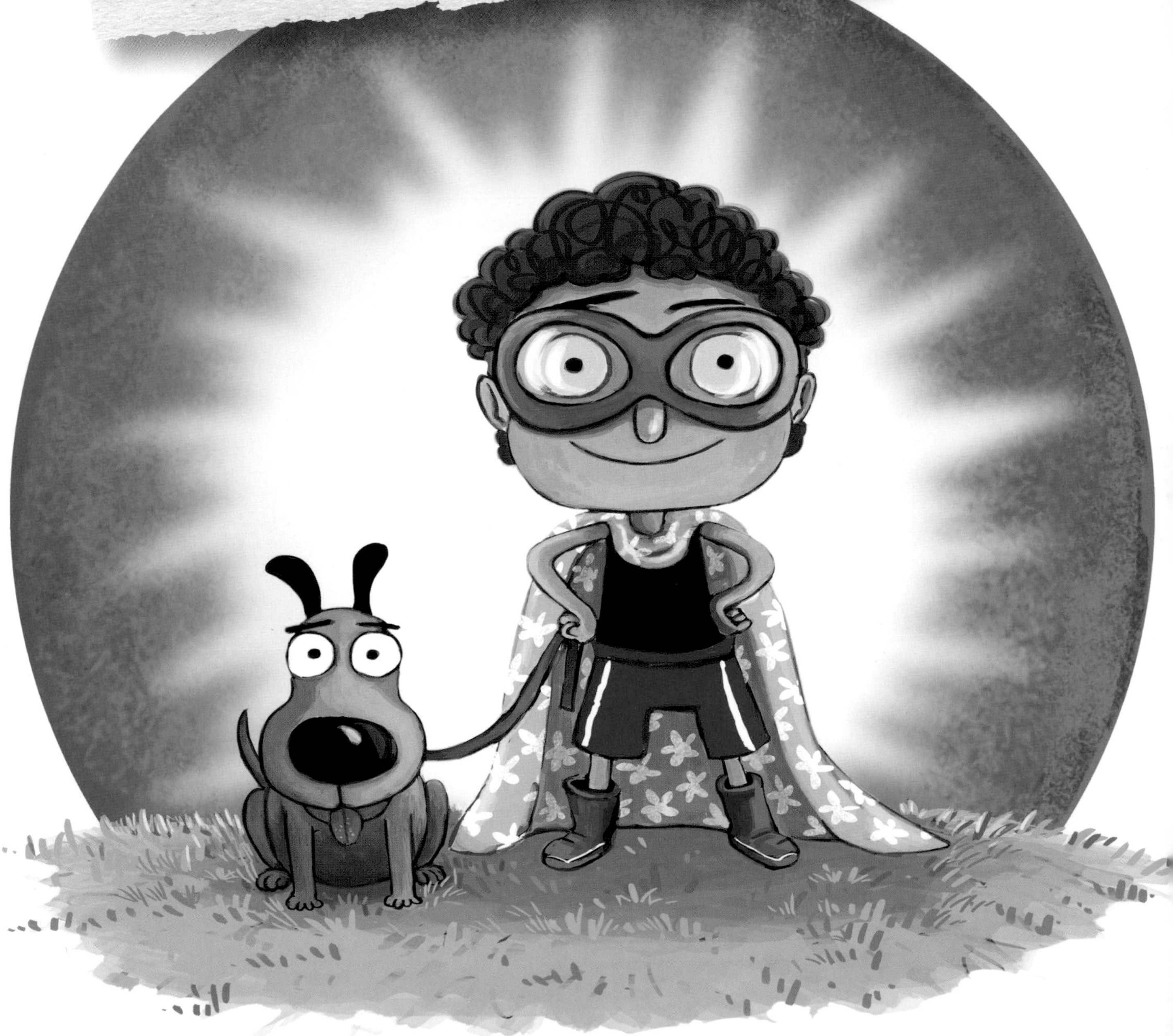

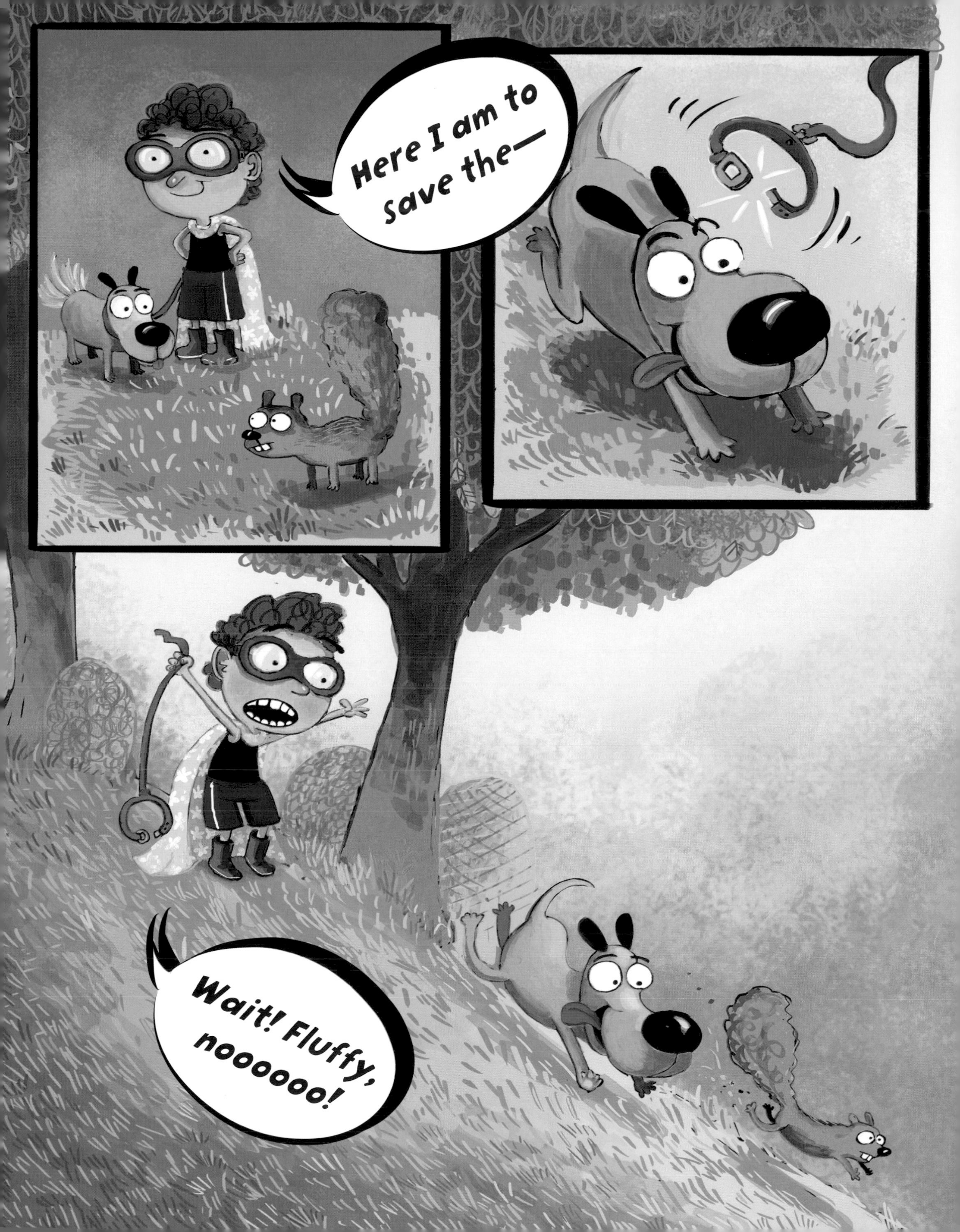
Here I am to save the—
Wait! Fluffy, noooooo!

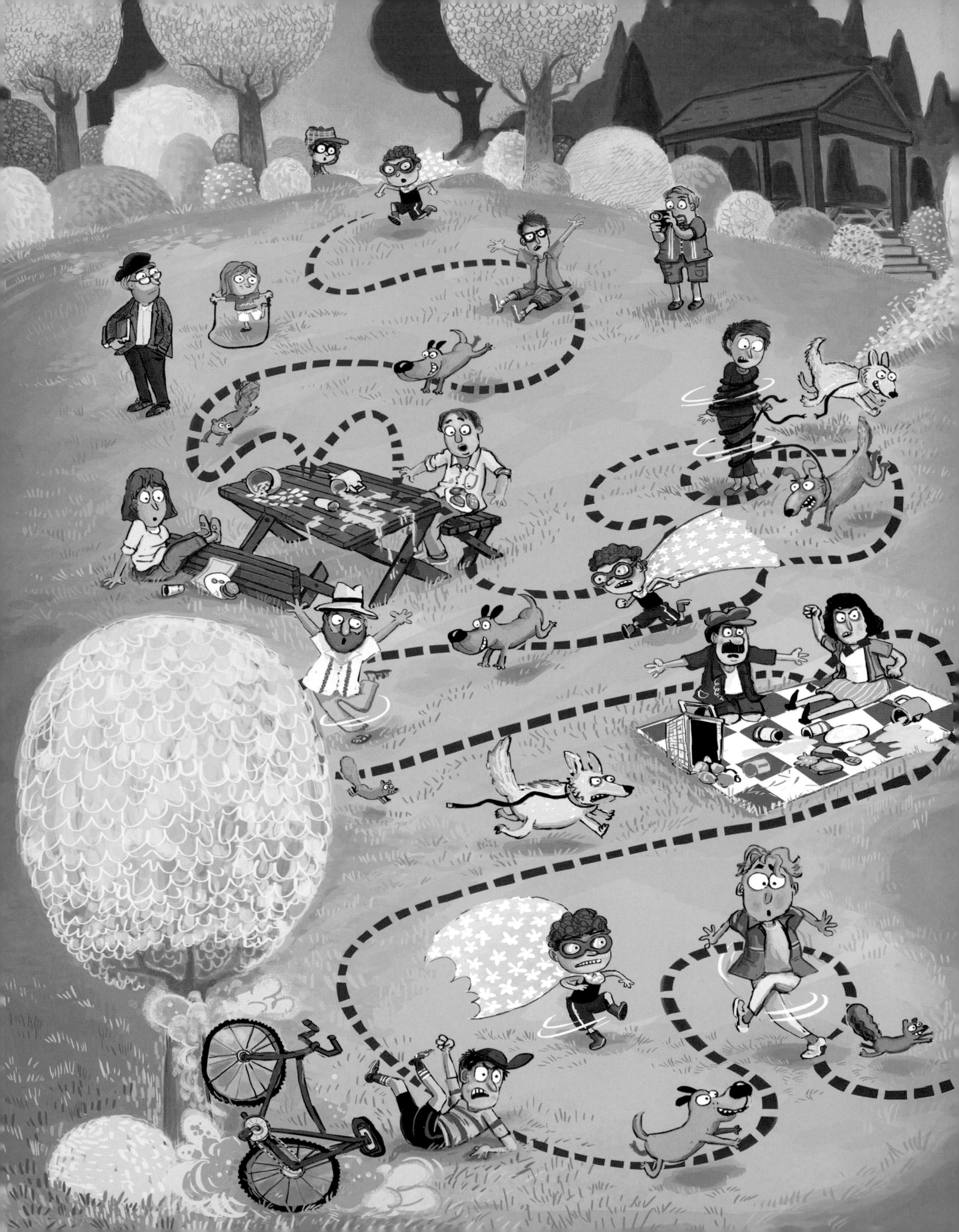

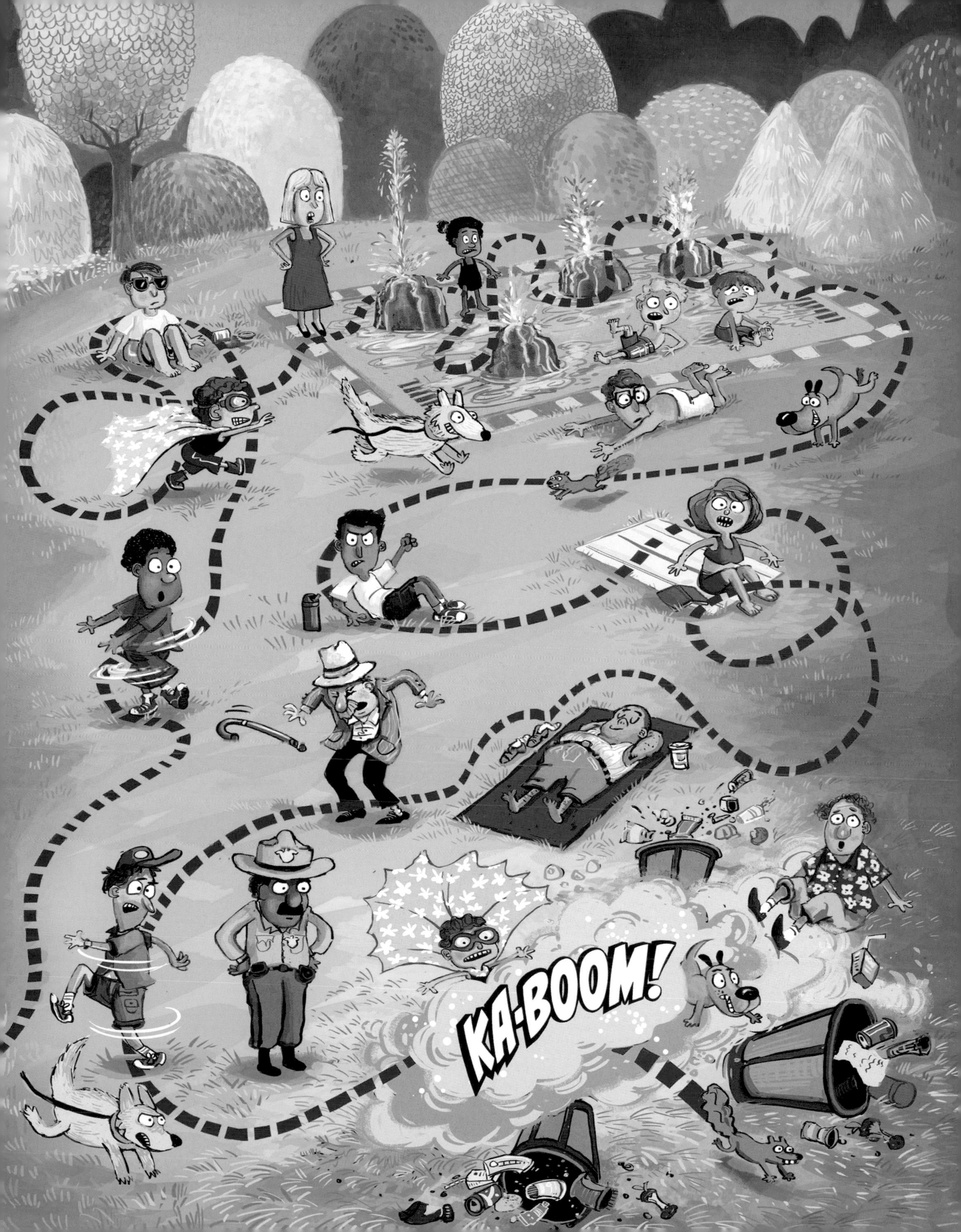
KA-BOOM!

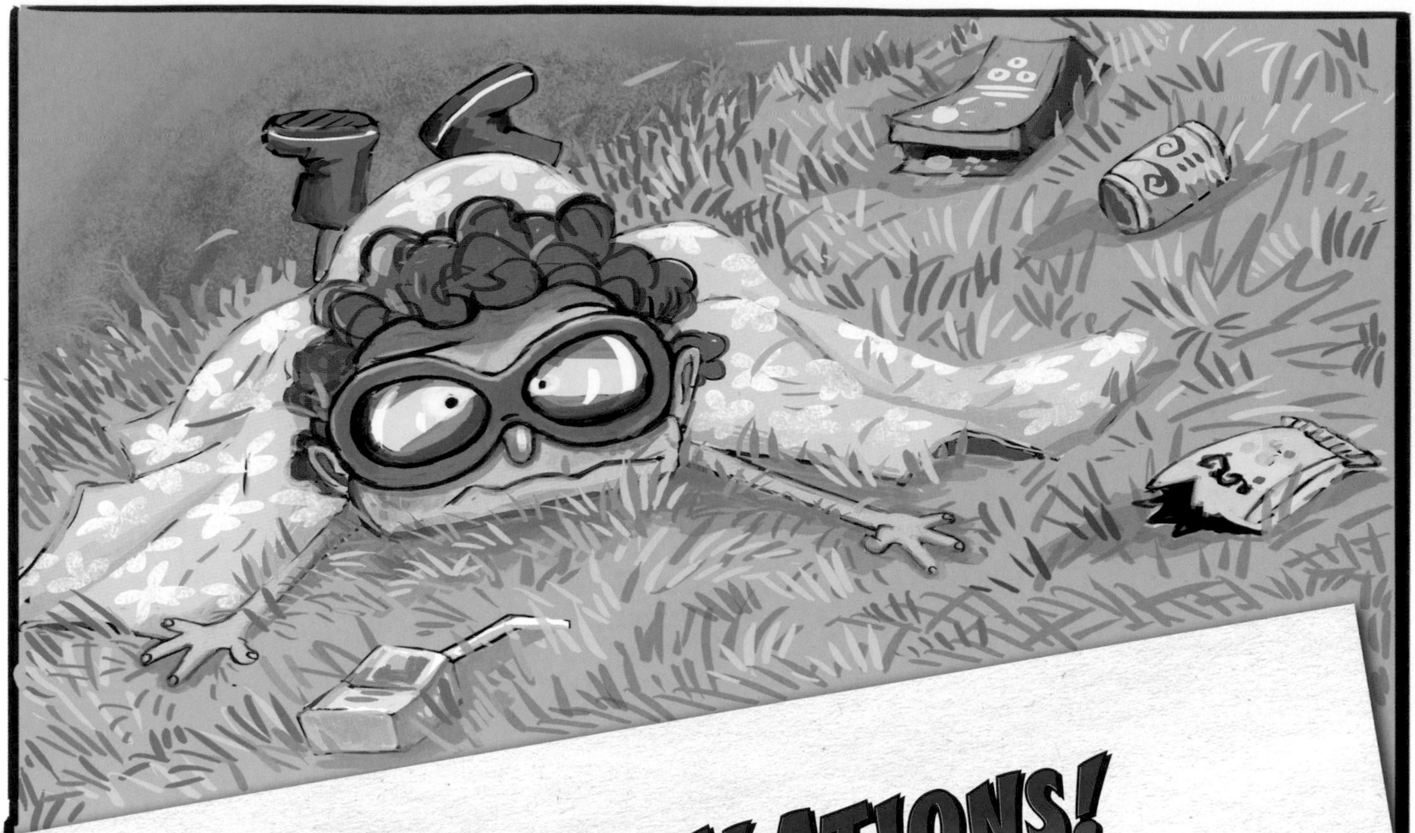

CONGRATULATIONS!

You have now completed the seven steps to becoming a hero.

You should feel super!

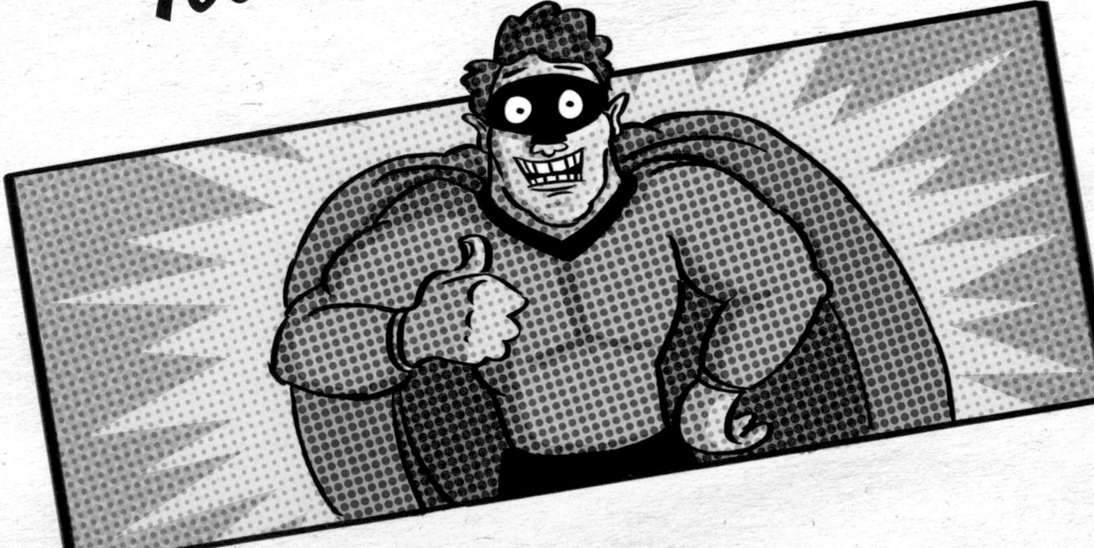

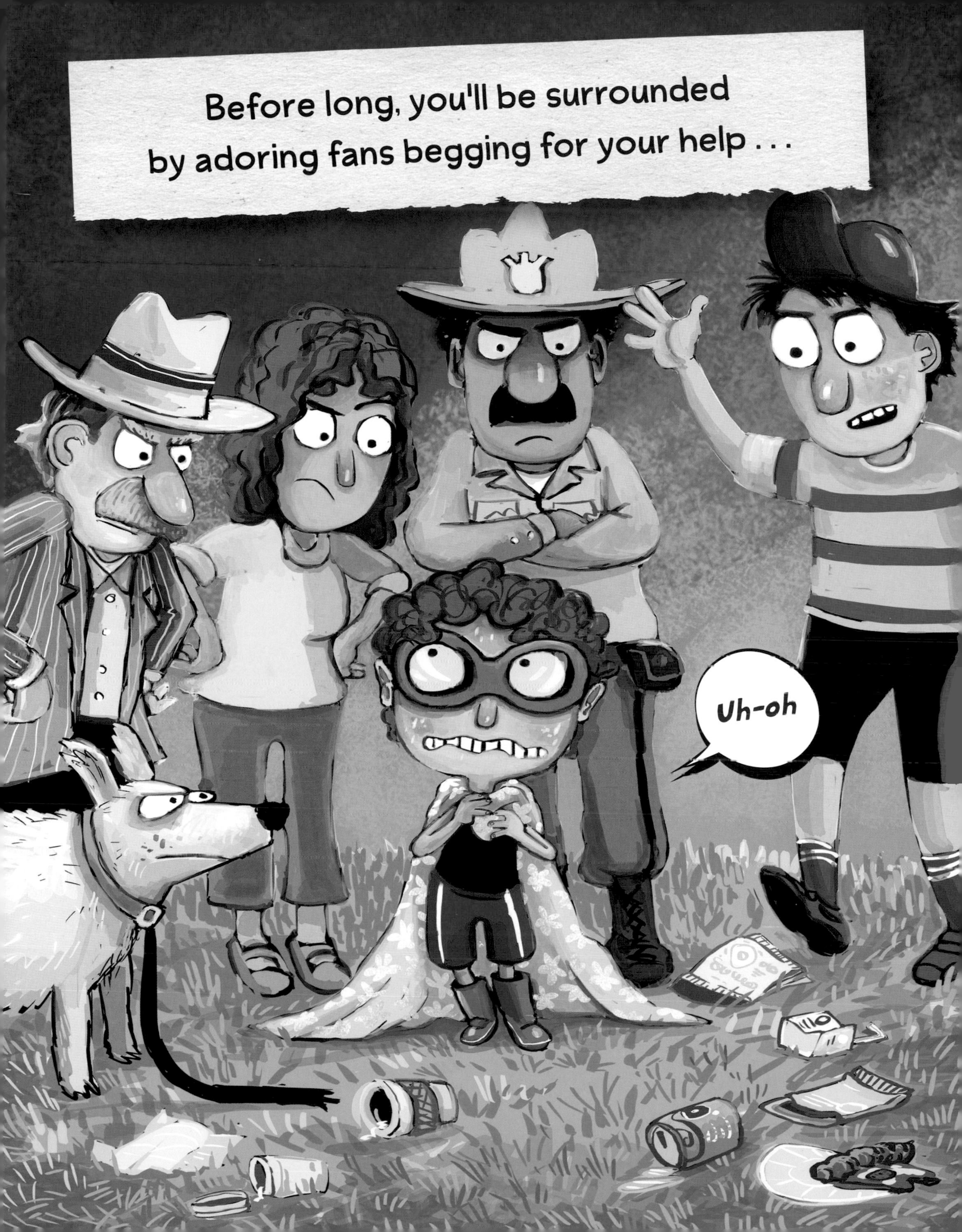
Before long, you'll be surrounded by adoring fans begging for your help . . .
Uh-oh

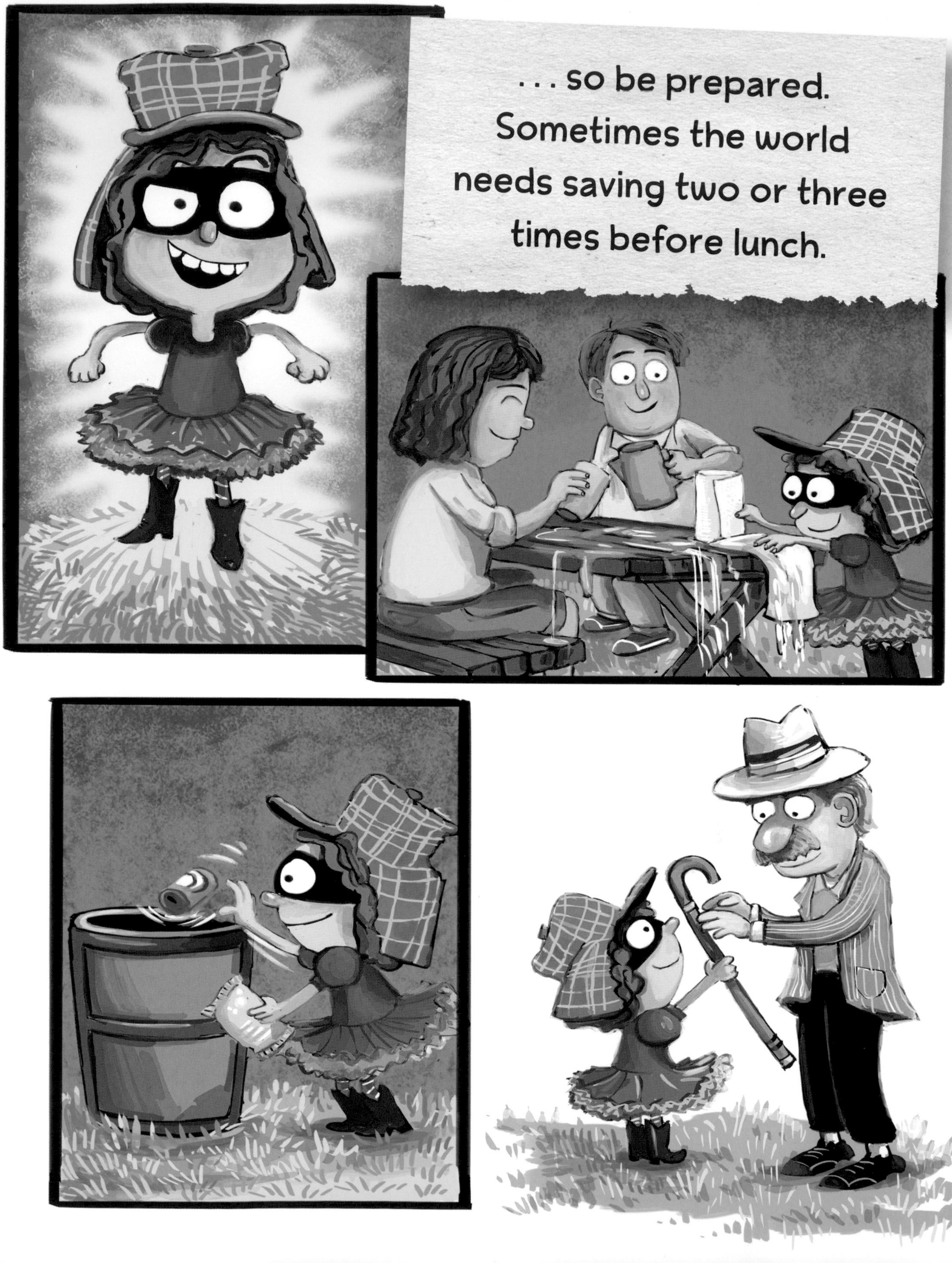
. . . so be prepared. Sometimes the world needs saving two or three times before lunch.

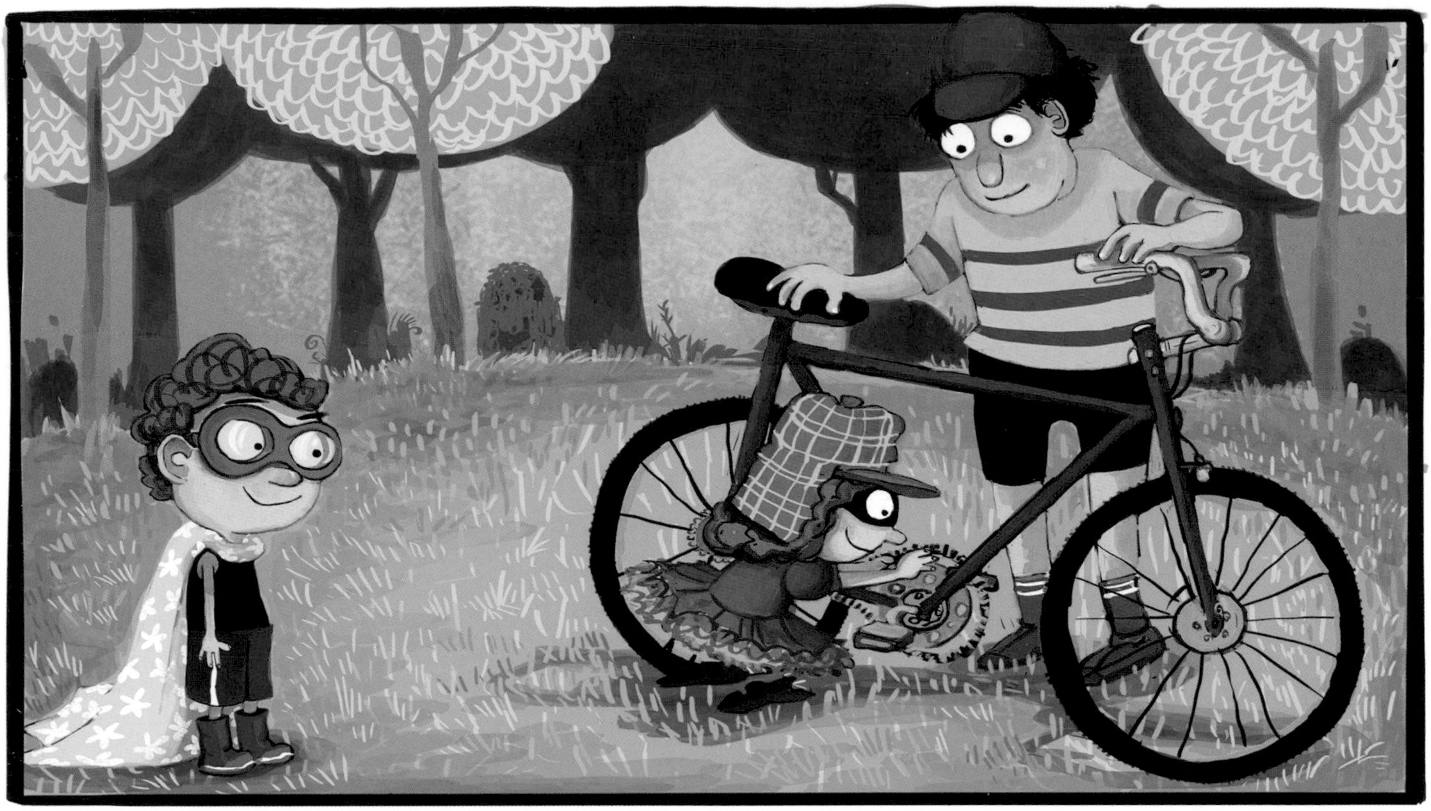
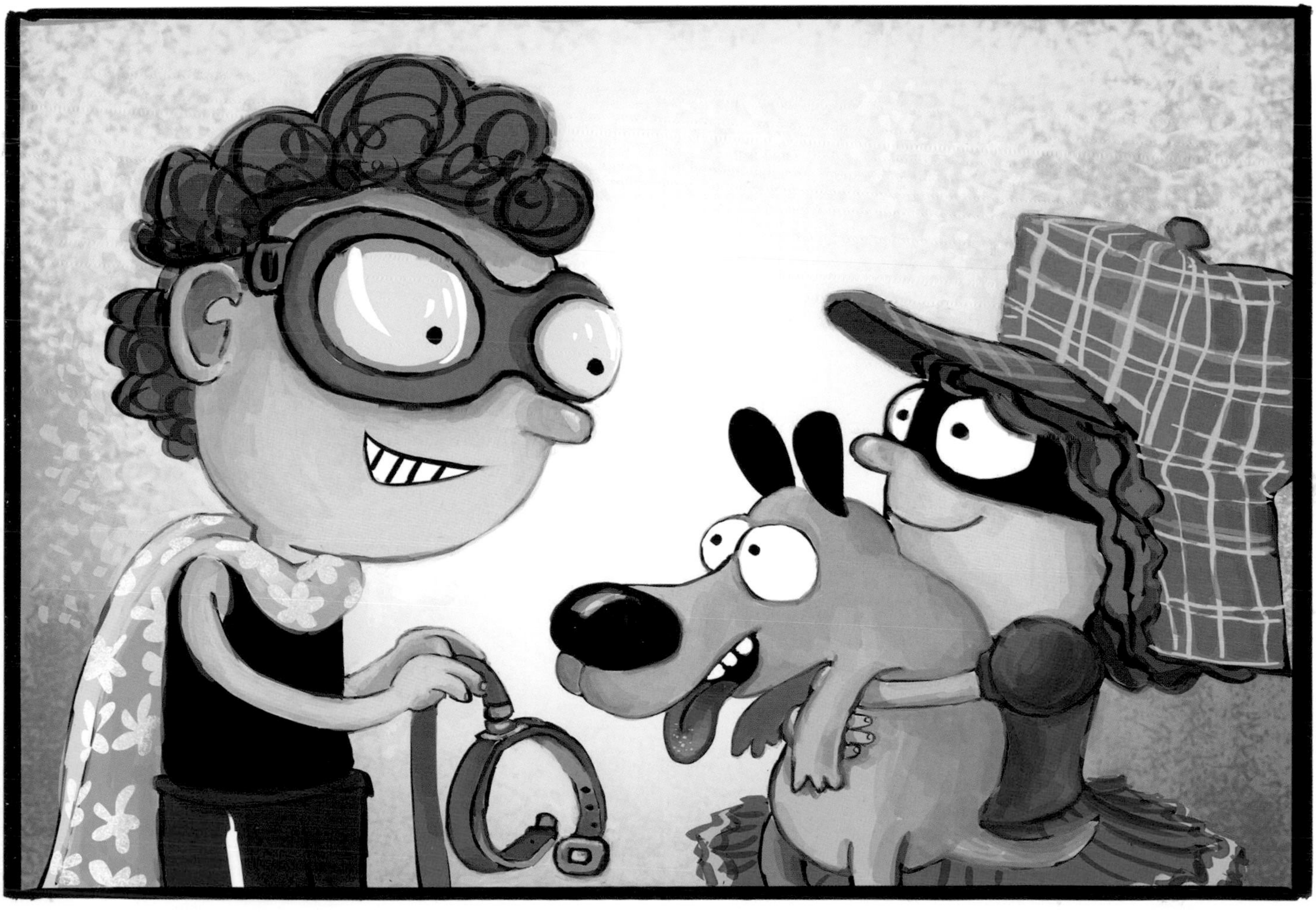

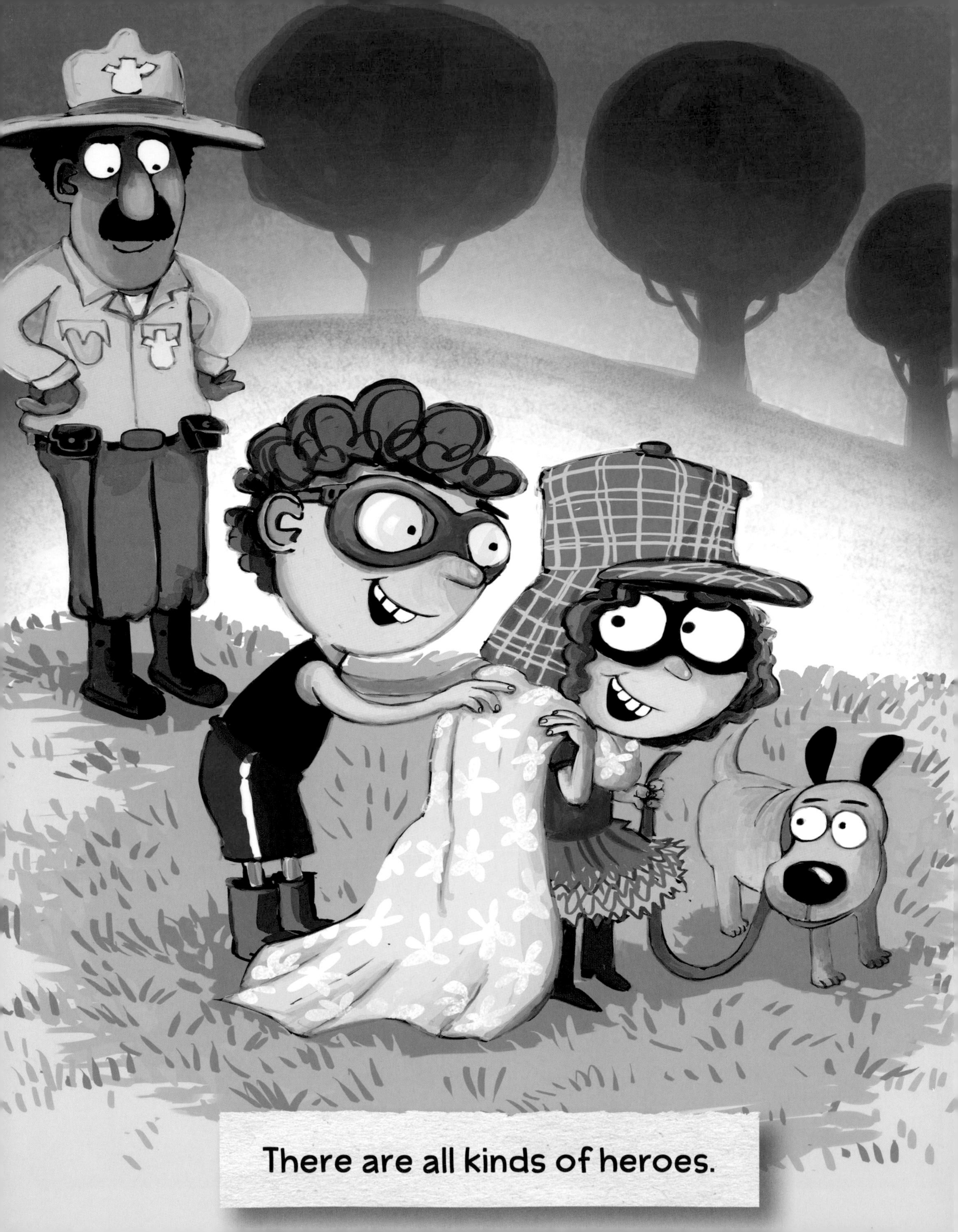

There are all kinds of heroes.

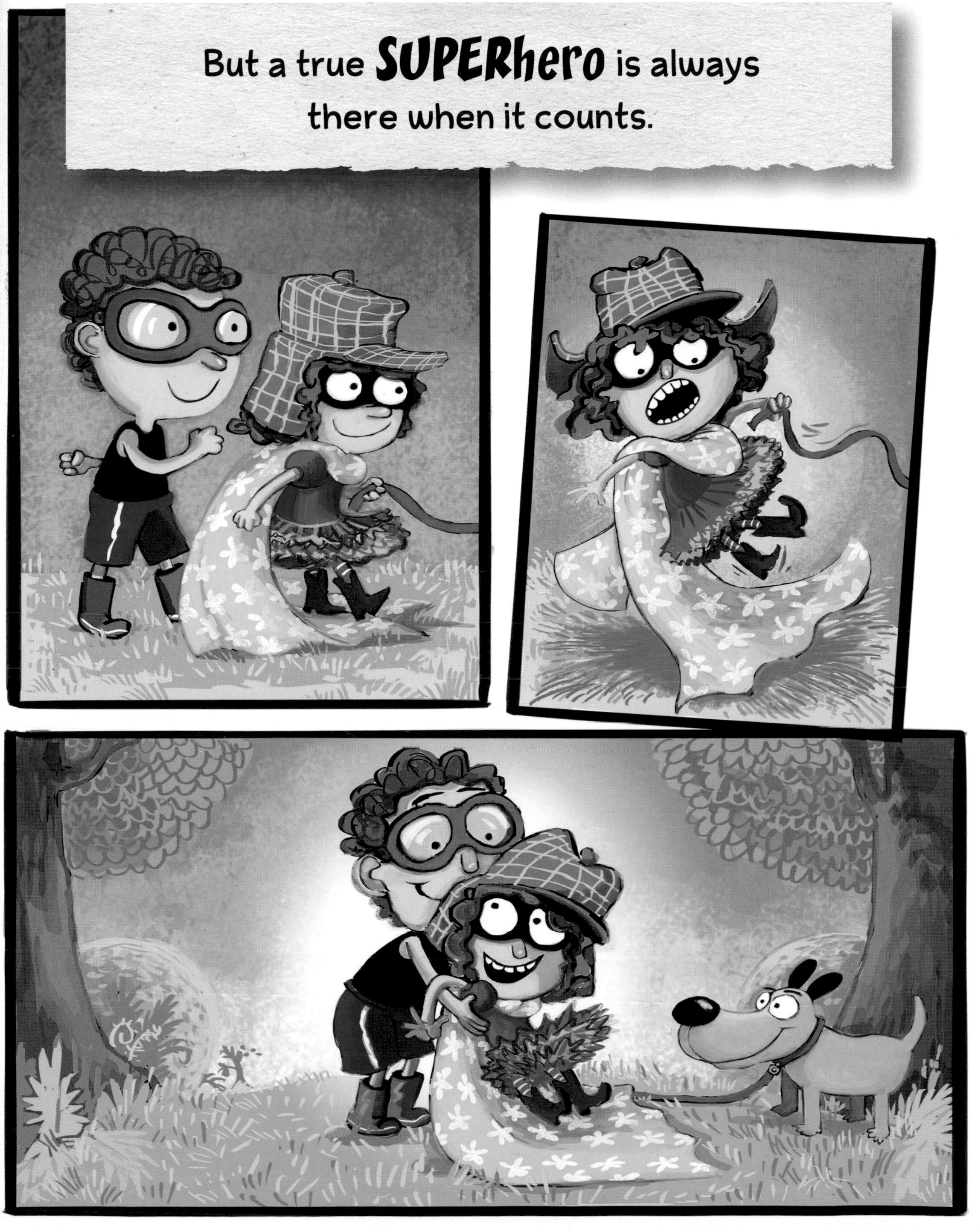
But a true **SUPERhero** is always there when it counts.

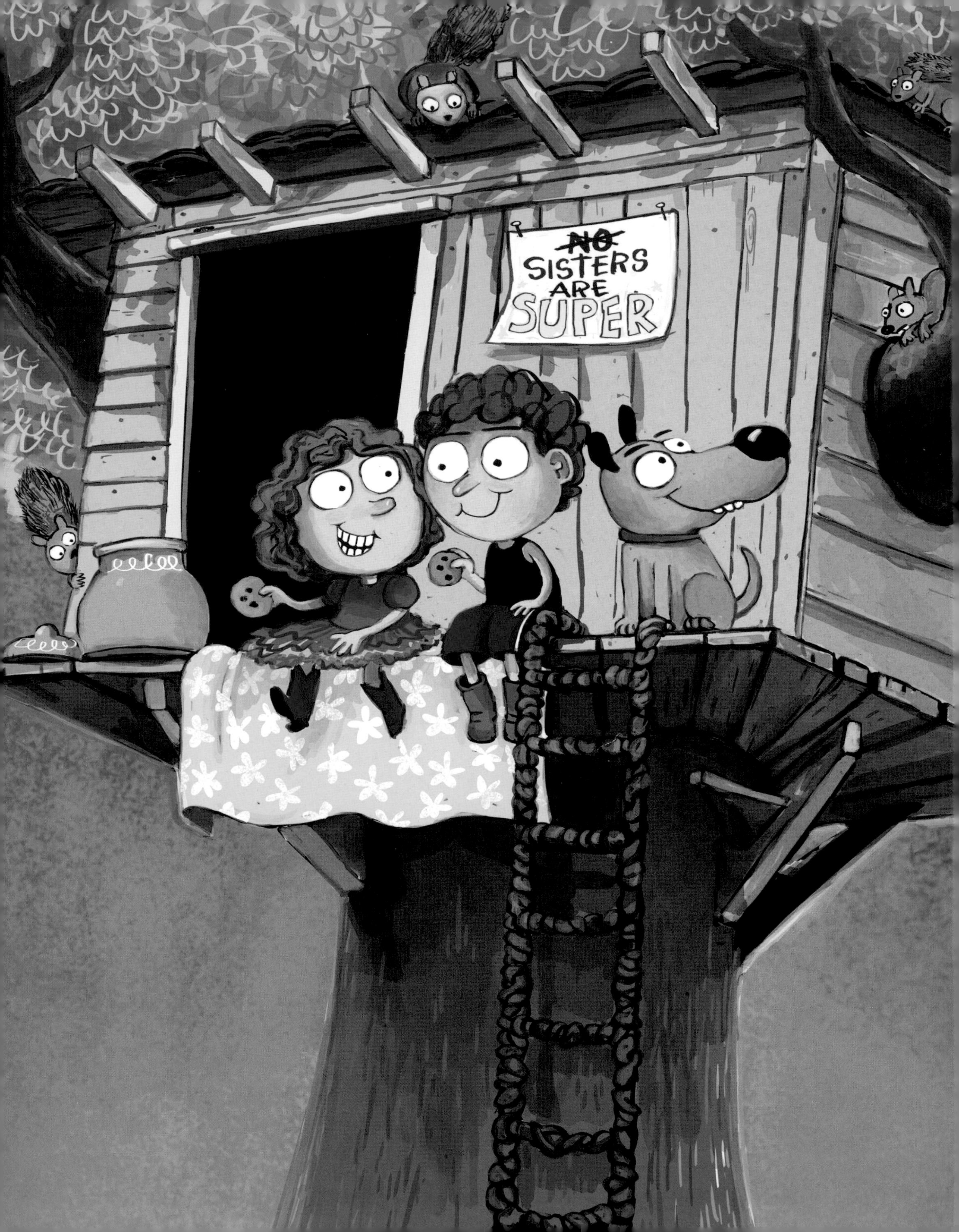

~~NO~~
SISTERS
ARE
SUPER

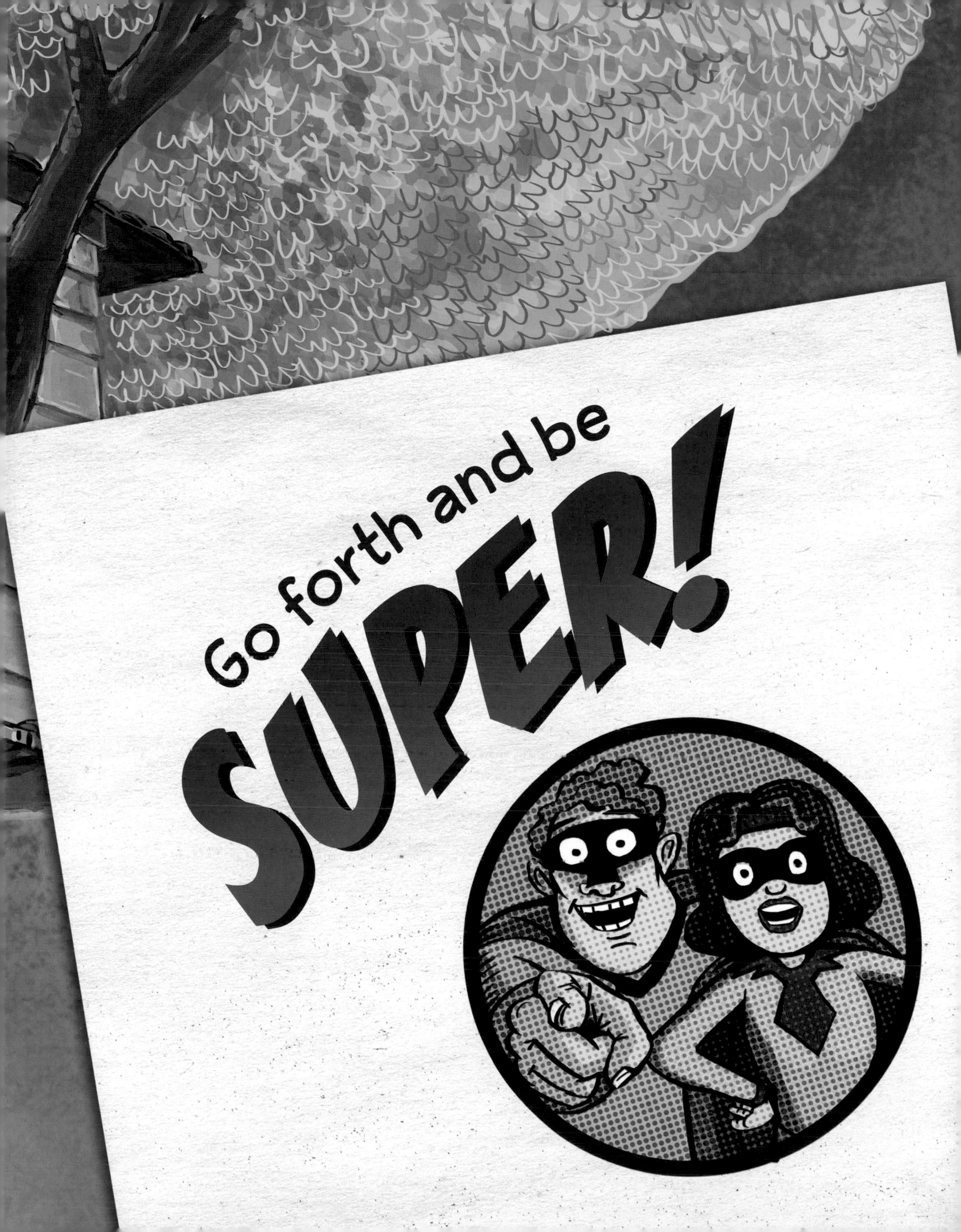
Go forth and be
SUPER!

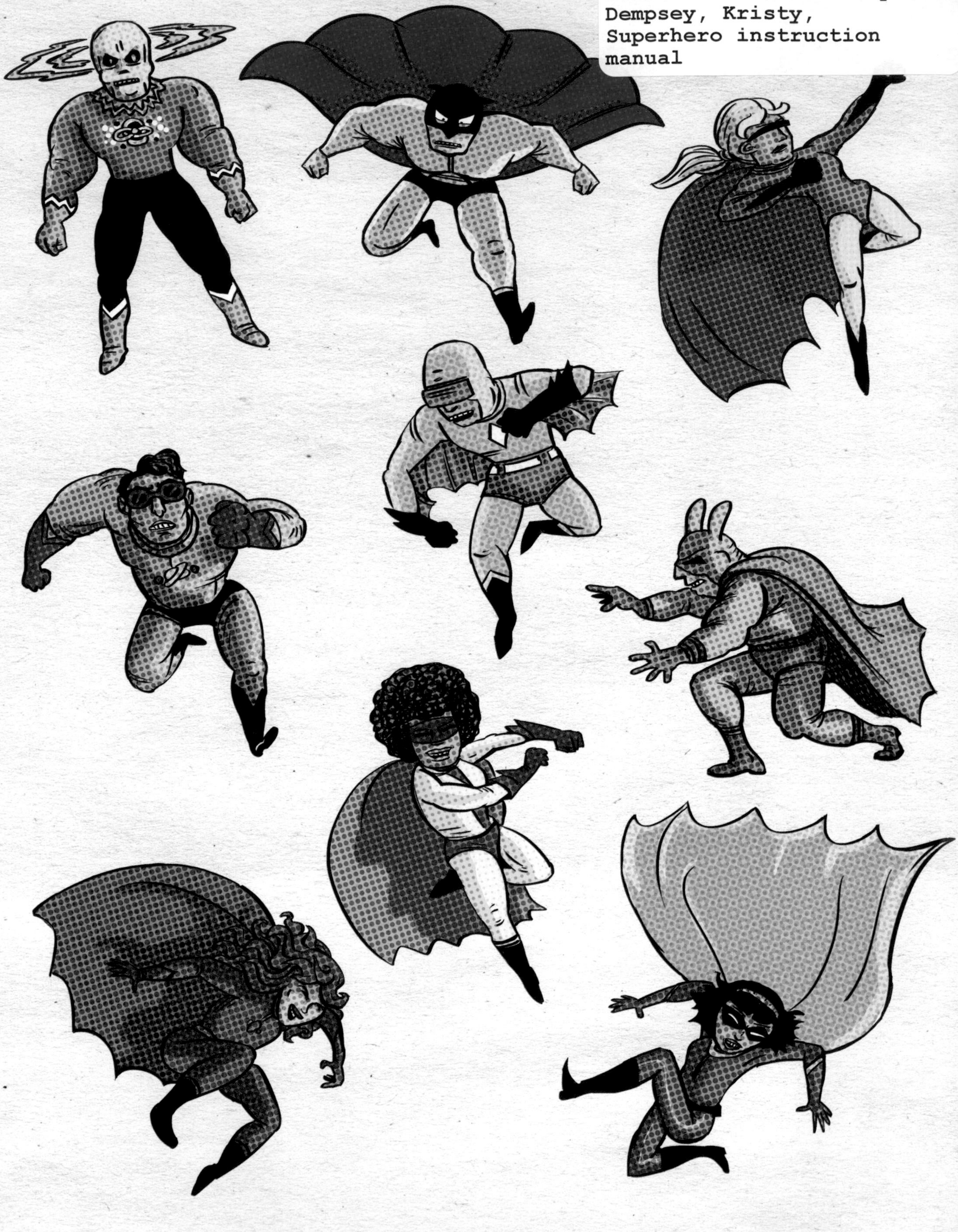